Praise for

A THOUSAND YEARS OF GOOD PRAYERS

"A subtle and original perspective on the latest chapter in China's turbulent history . . . Li is a valuable firsthand guide to this decade of mind-bending change. . . . [She] shows a light touch that, combined with her gift for characterization, saves her stories from turning into consciousness-raising exercises. . . . Poignant." —*The New York Times Book Review*

"Thoughtful, deceptively quiet, and always surprising, these seamless stories remind us that regardless of the society we inhabit, the most basic human emotions . . . transcend history and geography, and are universal, timeless, and endlessly mysterious." —*O: The Oprah Magazine*

"The stories in *A Thousand Years of Good Prayers* are both contemporary and universal, telling of love, death, and the joys and burdens of family against the backdrop of China's sudden modernity. . . . What's clear from this volume is that the delineations of [Li's] talent have only begun to come into view." —*Elle*

"Yiyun Li is a true storyteller. Great stories offer us the details of life on the riverbanks: birth, family, dinner and love, all framing the powerful flow of terror, death, political change, the river itself. *A Thousand Years of Good Prayers* is as grand an epic and as tenderly private as a reader could wish." —AMY BLOOM, author of *Come to Me*

A
THOUSAND
YEARS
OF
GOOD
PRAYERS

Yiyun Li

RANDOM HOUSE TRADE PAPERBACKS

NEW YORK

A
THOUSAND
YEARS
OF
GOOD
PRAYERS

STORIES

2006 Random House Trade Paperback Edition

Copyright © 2005 by Yiyun Li
Reading group guide copyright © 2006 by Random House, Inc.

Published in the United States by Random House Trade Paperbacks, an imprint of The Random House Publishing Group, a division of Random House, Inc., New York.

RANDOM HOUSE TRADE PAPERBACKS and colophon are trademarks of Random House, Inc.

RANDOM HOUSE READER'S CIRCLE and colophon is a trademark of Random House, Inc.

Originally published in hardcover in the United States by Random House, an imprint of The Random House Publishing Group, a division of Random House, Inc., in 2005.

"Immortality" and "Persimmons" were originally published in *The Paris Review*, in the Fall 2003 and Fall 2004 issues, respectively.

"Extra" was originally published in *The New Yorker*, in the December 22 & 29, 2003, issue.

"The Princess of Nebraska" was originally published in *Ploughshares*, in the Winter 2004 issue.

"Death Is Not a Bad Joke If Told the Right Way," was originally published in *Glimmer Train*, in the Spring 2005 issue.

"After a Life" was originally published in *Prospect*, in the April 2005 issue.

Excerpt from *Gold Boy, Emerald Girl* copyright © 2010 by Yiyun Li

Library of Congress Cataloging-in-Publication Data
Li, Yiyun.
A thousand years of good prayers / by Yiyun Li.
p.   cm.
ISBN 0-8129-7333-X
I. Title.
PL2946.Y59T46 2005
813'.6—dc22   2004062891

Printed in the United States of America

www.randomhousereaderscircle.com

10 12 14 16 18 19 17 15 13 11

Book design by Victoria Wong

For Dapeng

Contents

A
THOUSAND
YEARS
OF
GOOD
PRAYERS

Extra

GRANNY LIN WALKS IN THE STREET ON A NOvember afternoon with a stainless steel lunch pail in her hand. Inside the lunch pail is an official certificate from her working unit. "Hereby we confirm Comrade Lin Mei is honorably retired from Beijing Red Star Garment Factory," says the certificate in bright golden characters.

It does not say that Red Star Garment Factory has gone bankrupt or that, being honorably retired, Granny Lin will not receive her pension. Of course it will not provide such information, for these facts are simply not true. "Bankrupt" is the wrong word for a state-owned industry. "Internal reorganization" is what has been kindly omitted in the certificate. And, mind this, Granny Lin's pension is being withheld only temporarily. For how long, the factory has no further information to offer.

"There is always a road when you get into the mountain," Auntie Wang, Granny Lin's neighbor, says to her upon being informed of Granny Lin's situation.

"And there is a Toyota wherever there is a road." The second line of Toyota's commercial slips out before Granny realizes it.

"There you go, Granny Lin. I know you are an optimistic person. Stay positive and you will find your Toyota."

But where on earth can she find a way to replenish her dwindling savings? For a few days Granny Lin adds, subtracts, and divides, and she decides that her savings will run out in a year—in two years if she can skip a meal here and there, go to bed right after sunset, and stay bundled up so that she does not have to feed the insatiable stove extra coal balls through the long winter of northern China.

"Don't worry," Auntie Wang says the next time they meet each other at the market, looking down at the single radish Granny Lin has bought for her dinner, as plump as a Buddha, dwelling between her two palms. "You can always find someone and get married."

"Get married?" Granny Lin says, and blushes.

"Don't be so conservative, Granny Lin," Auntie Wang says. "How old are you?"

"Fifty-one."

"You are even younger than I am! I am fifty-eight, but I am not as old-fashioned as you. You know what? Young people no longer have a monopoly on marriage."

"Don't make me a clown," Granny Lin says.

"I am serious, Granny Lin. There are so many old widowers in the city. I am sure there are rich and sick ones who need someone to take care of them."

"You mean, I can find a caretaker's position for old people?" Granny Lin asks.

Auntie Wang sighs and pokes Granny Lin's forehead with a finger. "Use your brain. Not a caretaker but a wife. That way, you can at least inherit some cash when your husband dies."

Granny Lin gasps. She has never had a husband in her

life, and the prospect of a dead husband frightens her. Yet Auntie Wang makes the decision for her right there and then, between two fish stands, and in a short time she finds Granny Lin a match.

"Seventy-six. High blood pressure and diabetes. Wife just died. Living alone in a three-bedroom flat. Pension two thousand yuan a month. Both sons married and earning good money in the government," Auntie Wang says, surprised that Granny Lin remains unimpressed. "Come on, Granny Lin, where else can you find such a good husband? The old man will die in no time, and the sons are so rich they won't mind sparing some of the old man's savings for you. Let me tell you, this is the most eligible family, as far as I know. Their doorsill has been worn away by the feet of the matchmakers. But of all the possible wives, they are interested only in you. Why? Because you are never married and you have no children. By the way, Granny Lin, how come you aren't married? You never told us the reason."

Granny Lin opens and then closes her mouth. "It just happens," she says.

"You don't have to tell me if you don't want to. Anyway, they don't want someone who has a litter of children and grandchildren. I wouldn't trust such a stepmother, either. Who can guarantee that she won't steal from the old man for her children? But you are the best. I have told them that, were there one honest person left on earth, it would be you, Granny Lin. What are you hesitating for?"

"Why don't they hire someone to take care of him?" Granny Lin asks, thinking of the two sons who might soon become her stepchildren. "Won't it be cheaper in the long run?"

"Do you not know what those young girls from the nanny

market are like? They are lazy, and they steal money—husbands, too, if they are hired by young couples. They leave the old people sitting in their own shit all day long. To hire such a girl? Ugh. It would only push him to death quicker."

Granny Lin has to agree that, indeed, an older woman as a wife is a wise choice. Accompanied by Auntie Wang, Granny Lin goes to the interview with the two sons and their wives. An hour of questioning later, the two sons exchange a look, and ask if Granny Lin needs some time to consider the marriage offer. Not having much to think about, she moves into her new home in a week. Her husband, Old Tang, is sicker than she has thought. "Alzheimer's," a daughter-in-law tells her at their wedding dinner.

Granny Lin nods, not knowing what the disease is but guessing that it has something to do with the brain. She supports her husband with both hands and leads him to the table, sitting him down and wiping away the drool from his chin.

GRANNY LIN BECOMES a wife, a mother, and a grandmother. She no longer remembers in what year of her life people started to call her Granny Lin instead of Auntie Lin; unmarried women, people believe, age faster. It does not matter anymore, because she feels quite qualified for her name.

Every week, one of the sons stops by and checks on Old Tang, leaving enough money for the next week. Old Tang is a quiet man, sitting in his chair by the window, immersed in his bottomless silence. Once in a while, he asks Granny Lin about his wife, and, as instructed by the two sons, Granny Lin replies that the wife is improving in the hospital and will be home in no time. But before she replies Old Tang seems to have forgotten his question, and goes back to his meditation without any sign of having heard Granny Lin. She waits for more questions that never come, and eventually gives up. She turns up the volume of the television and shuffles around the house, sweeping and dusting and wiping and washing, but the time arrives earlier each day when she finishes the housework. Then she sits down on the couch and watches the daytime soap operas. Unlike the twelve-inch television Granny Lin used to own, which required her to make a trip across the room every time she needed to change channels (and all together she got six channels through the antenna made of two steel chopsticks), Old Tang's set is a monster with scores of channels, which all obey a small remote control. Dazed by all the choices she has, and by the ease of moving from one selection to another, Granny Lin soon finds that the machine does her no good. No matter what program she is watching, there is always the nagging worry that she is missing a more interesting one. Several days into her new life, Granny Lin is stunned to discover that she is no longer addicted to television, as she has been in the past ten years. Does marriage have such revolutionary power that a long-established habit can be overthrown in such a short time?

Granny Lin sighs and clicks off the television. Old Tang does not notice the silence flooding the room. She realizes then that the television is not to blame. It is because of Old Tang's presence that she cannot focus. She picks up an old magazine and peeks at Old Tang from behind the pages. Ten minutes grows into twenty minutes, and she continues looking at him as he insists on not meeting her gaze. She has an odd suspicion that Old Tang is not ill. He knows she is there, and he is observing her secretly. He knows that his wife of fifty-four years has left him for good and that Granny Lin is his new wife, but he refuses to acknowledge her. He pretends to have lost his mind and expects her to play along as if she were a hired caretaker. But Granny Lin decides not to concede. He is her husband; she is his wife. Their marriage certificate is secure under her pillow. If Old Tang is testing her patience, she is ready to prove it to him; it is a tug-of-war that Granny Lin is determined to win. She puts down the magazine and looks boldly into Old Tang's face, trying to outstare Old Tang. Minutes stretch into an hour, and all of a sudden Granny Lin awakens in a dread that she, too, is losing her mind. She drags her body out of the couch and stretches, feeling the small cracking of her arthritic joints. She looks down at Old Tang, and he is still a statue. Indeed, he is a sick man, she thinks, and feels the shame of having cast rootless doubt on Old Tang, a man as defenseless as a newborn baby. She walks to the kitchen quickly and comes back with a glass of milk. "Milk time," she says, patting Old Tang's cheek until he starts to swallow.

Three times a day, Granny Lin gives Old Tang an insulin shot. Only then does she catch a glimpse of the life left in Old Tang, the small flinch of the muscle when she pushes the needle into his arm. Sometimes a small bead of blood appears after she draws the needle out, and she wipes it away with her fingertip instead of a cotton ball, entranced by the strange sensation that his blood is seeping into her body.

SEVERAL TIMES A day Granny Lin bathes Old Tang: in the morning and before bedtime, and whenever he wets or dirties himself. The private bathroom is what Granny Lin likes best about her marriage. For all her life, she has used public bathrooms, fighting with other slippery bodies for the luke-warm water drizzling from the rusty showers. Now that she has a bathroom all to herself, she never misses any chance to use it.

Old Tang is the only man Granny Lin has seen in full nakedness. The first time she undressed him, she could not help stealing a look now and then at the penis, nestled in a thinning bush. She wondered what it had looked like in its younger years, but right away chased the unclean thought from her mind. The frail nakedness filled her heart with a tenderness she had never experienced, and she has since tended his body with motherly hands.

One evening in late February, Granny Lin leads Old Tang to the plastic chair in the middle of the bathroom. She un-buttons his pajamas and he bends his arms at her guidance, his head leaning on her shoulder blade. She removes the nozzle and sprays warm water on his body, putting one hand on his forehead so that the water does not get into his eyes.

Granny Lin is squatting on the floor and massaging Old Tang's legs when he touches her shoulder with his palm. She looks up and he is gazing into her eyes. She gives out a cry and backs away from him.

"Who are you?" Old Tang says.

"Old Tang," Granny Lin says. "Is it you?"

"Who are you? Why are you here?"

"I live here," Granny Lin says. She sees an unnatural lu-cidity in Old Tang's eyes, and feels her heart fall. Such a mo-ment of clarity happens only before a nearing death. Granny Lin had seen the same light two years earlier in her father's eyes, hours before he passed away. She thinks of rushing out to call a doctor, but her feet are locked on the floor, and her eyes are locked in his eyes.

"I don't know you. Who are you?"

Granny Lin looks down at herself. She is wearing a bright yellow plastic poncho and a pair of grass green rubber boots, her outfit for the bath time. "I am your wife," she says.

"You are not my wife. My wife is Sujane. Where is Sujane?"

"Sujane is no longer with us. I'm your new wife."

"You're lying," Old Tang says, and stands up. "Sujane is in the hospital."

"No," Granny Lin says. "They lied to you."

Old Tang does not hear her. He pushes Granny Lin, and his arms are suddenly strong. Granny Lin clutches him, but he is wild with uncontrollable force. She lets go of his hands, not knowing why she needs to fight with her husband over a dead woman. But he is still wrestling with the air and, two steps away, slips down in a puddle of soapy water.

Nobody pays attention to Granny Lin at the funeral. She sits in a corner and listens to the men and women who come up to talk about Old Tang's life: an accomplished physicist and a great teacher, a loving husband, father, and grandfather. The speakers finish and shake the family members' hands, ignoring her at the end of the line.

I did not kill him, Granny Lin imagines herself telling every person there. He was dying before the fall. But she does not tell the truth to anyone, and instead admits her negligence. Nobody would believe her anyway, for she alone saw the light in his eyes, the last glimmer before the eternal night, as it is called, the brief moment of lucidity before the end.

. . .

GRANNY LIN DOES not get a penny from Old Tang's savings. She has looked after Old Tang for only two months, and has, in many of the relatives' minds, killed him with her carelessness. She does not blame the two sons. She can think only of their loss, a thousand times more painful than her own. When one of them suggests a job in a private boarding school that is run by his friend, Granny Lin almost weeps out of gratitude.

Situated in a mountain resort in a western suburb of Beijing, Mei-Mei Academy takes pride in being among the first private schools in the country. It occupies one of the few four-storied buildings that were allowed to be constructed in the area. ("Connections, connections," the chef tells Granny Lin the day she arrives—how else could the school have gained the permit if not for its powerful trustees?) Private schools, like all private businesses, are sprouting up across the country like bamboo shoots after the first spring rain. Relatives of the Communist Party leaders are being transformed overnight into business owners, their faces appearing on national TV as representatives of the new proletariat entrepreneurs.

Granny Lin cannot imagine a better life now that she becomes a maid at the academy. Every meal is a banquet. Meat and fish are abundant. Vegetables are greener than Granny Lin remembers from her market days. Everything is produced by a small organic farm that serves the president and the premier and their families—so the chef informs Granny Lin.

Sometimes Granny Lin feels sad at seeing so much good food go into the garbage. She begins to come late to her meals, waiting until the students finish theirs. Throughout the dining hall, untouched vegetables are left withering on the plates; shipwrecked fishes lie flat on their half-gnawed bellies. Granny Lin spoons the leftovers onto her plate and dreams of having an express shuttle running between the school and the city every day, taking the unconsumed food to her old neighbors.

Eating such good food without working hard is a sin. In addition to the laundry and dorm cleaning assigned to her, Granny Lin takes on other duties. She gets up early in the morning and opens the classroom windows to let in fresh mountain air. She sweeps and mops the terrazzo floor. She dusts and wipes the students' desks. She makes sure everything is meticulous, even though the janitor has cleaned the classrooms the night before. Sometimes, when there is still time before the wake-up bell, she leaves the school and takes a walk in the mountains. The morning fog is damp on her skin and her hair, and birds she has never seen in the city sing in a chorus. At such moments, Granny Lin feels overwhelmed by her good fortune. The years in the factory seem a distant dream now, and she no longer remembers what her life was like when she walked through the morning smog expelled by the coal stoves and bargained in the market for vegetables puffed up by chemical fertilizers.

Often Granny Lin gathers an armful of wildflowers on her walk: mountain orchids, pearl cherries, jade barrettes. She arranges the flowers in vases for the six classrooms, one for each grade, but such a delicacy rarely lasts beyond the first period. Boys of all ages pelt one another with the flowers; the boy whose lips touch the flowers is called a sissy. Girls of the upper grades pull the petals off and bury them in a mound in the school yard, their fingers ruthless and their faces shrouded with a sad seriousness.

. . .

THE SCHOOL IS growing. Every month a few new students arrive. Granny Lin is stunned by the parents' wealth, the ease with which they pay the initiation fee of twenty thousand yuan and another twenty thousand for the first year of tuition and room and board.

In the third month of Granny Lin's stay, the school celebrates its one hundredth student with a feast. Kang, the boy who draws the lucky number, is six years old. Unlike the other students, who come from the city, he was sent from a nearby province. A few days into his stay, the teachers and the staff members have all heard his story. Kang's grandfather used to be the leader of a big People's commune in his home province, and his father has become one of the top agricultural entrepreneurs in northern China.

"I thought farmers liked to keep their sons at home," Granny Lin says to Mrs. Du, a dorm mother, as they search for the foul-smelling socks under the mattresses. "They can almost stand up and walk by themselves" is how Mrs. Du describes the stiff socks that have been worn for too long.

"Not when he is the son of a disfavored wife," Mrs. Du says. "An extra is what he is."

"Are the parents divorced?"

"Who knows? But the father does have another wife, or a concubine. What's the difference? The boy's mother is no longer needed in the family, and the child has to go, too."

The thought of the boy, who is so small and occupies almost no space at all in the world yet who is still in other people's way and has to be got rid of, saddens Granny Lin. She starts to look for the boy among the crowd. His clothes, of the same brand names as those that the other students wear, look wrong on him. Too large, too new, too trendy, the clothes do not belong to him any more than he belongs to the school. His face and hands always seem in need of a thorough wash, but after Granny Lin herself has tended to them several times, she has to agree that it is not the child's or the dorm mother's fault.

In the second week, Kang starts to come to the laundry room during the afternoon activity time. "Granny, what's this?" he asks one day while Granny Lin is massaging some baby lotion into his cheeks.

"Something that will make you a city boy," Granny Lin says.

"Granny, where do you live?"

"I live here."

"But before you came here? Where is your husband's home?"

Granny Lin thinks for a moment. "In the city," she says.

"What's the city like? My mom said she'd take me to see the city."

"Where is your mom?" Granny Lin asks, holding her breath and trying to make her heart beat less loudly. The boy seems not to notice.

"She is at home."

"Your father's home?"

"My grandfather's home. My new mom lives in my father's home."

"What's your new mom like? Is she pretty?"

"Yes."

"Is she good to you?"

"Yes."

"Do you like her?"

"Yes."

"Do you like your mom also? More than your new mom?"

Granny Lin asks. She turns around to see whether anyone is walking past the laundry room in the hallway. She feels like a thief.

The boy, too, turns around nervously. He then comes closer and circles his arms around Granny Lin's neck, his mouth to Granny Lin's ear, his hot breath touching her earlobe. "Granny, I'll tell you a secret. Don't tell anyone."

"I won't."

"My mom said she would come and get me back one day."

"When?"

"She said soon."

"When did she say it?"

"Before my new mom moved in."

"When was that?"

"Last year."

"Have you seen your mom since then?"

"No, but she said she'd come soon, if I don't make my dad and my new mom angry," Kang says. "Granny, do you think the guards will let her in when she comes?"

"I'm sure they will," Granny Lin says. The boy smells like a mixture of baby lotion, fresh laundry, and clean sweat. It reminds Granny Lin of Old Tang after his bath, the way a dear person smells good. The thought makes Granny Lin's lips go dry, and she feels the boy's arms on her neck, hot and sticky.

ON FRIDAY AFTERNOONS, the parking lot outside the school gate is full of luxury cars. Chauffeurs and nannies come, and sometimes the parents themselves show up. Teachers and dorm mothers stand inside the gate, pointing out to one another who is the daughter-in-law of a power figure in the government and who has appeared in the latest hit movie.

Kang is the only child who stays for the weekend. His father has paid the extra fee for the weekend care and has promised to come for him at the end of the semester. Sometimes Granny Lin wonders if the father will ever come and what will become of Kang if no one picks him up when summer comes. Will he be able to stay with her at the school? Then she wonders if she herself will be allowed to stay and, if not, where she will spend the two months before she is allowed back in September.

After the last student is picked up every weekend, the teachers and the dorm mothers leave on a shuttle bus for the city. Apart from the two guards, Granny Lin is the only one who stays, and she has cheerfully agreed to take care of Kang.

They stand side by side at the school gate and wave at the bus. Both sigh with relief once it is gone. Kang darts across the yard to the activity room, flipping through the picture books as fast as he can, eager to get to the next one. Granny Lin comes in and sits down at his side, stroking his hair and watching him laugh to himself. When he finishes all the new books, they go out together and play in the yard, Granny Lin pushing him in the swing until it is flying so high that Kang screams with excitement and fear.

When the weather is nice, they take long walks in the mountains. Weekend tourists swarm into the area, but Granny Lin and Kang are the only two people who do not worry about missing the bus or getting stuck in a traffic jam. They walk hand in hand, Kang's palm touching Granny Lin's palm, both sweating. Granny Lin tells old tales about flowers and grasses. When she runs out of stories, she makes up new ones.

After dinner, Granny Lin leads Kang to the bathroom. She waits outside with a towel and his pajamas, and he sings in the shower the song about the red dragonfly she has taught him. Always he shouts to Granny Lin after the first two minutes, asking if he can come out now. She replies it would be good if he could stay in the shower for another five minutes. The boy goes on singing, his voice pure and perfect.

Often, without turning off the water, Kang jumps out of the stall at Granny Lin. She pretends to be startled and screams, and he giggles and runs off before she can wrap the towel around his dripping body.

At night, as he sleeps, he mumbles in his dreams, his arms and legs thrown to all four directions on the blanket. Granny Lin tucks him in and watches him for a long time, the unfamiliar warmth swelling inside her. She wonders if this is what people call falling in love, the desire to be with someone for every minute of the rest of her life so strong that sometimes she is frightened of herself.

GRANNY LIN IS not the first person to have noticed the missing socks. The dorm mothers, for two weeks in a row, tell her that the girls are complaining that their favorite socks are disappearing in the laundry. Granny Lin knows then what has happened to the socks. A few times, she has seen Kang clutch a girl's unwashed sock. He drops it into the basket when he realizes that she is watching him.

The next weekend, while Kang is playing a computer game in the activity room, Granny Lin searches his bed. She finds nothing under the mattress, where the kids usually hide things. She folds back the blanket. She picks up the pillow and unzips the pillowcase, and sees five socks inside, rolled up into small bundles like newborn bunnies.

Granny Lin unrolls them: young girls' socks with flowered patterns or cartoon animals. She thinks of putting them in her own pocket, but stops at the thought of Kang groping in the pillowcase for the socks, something dear to him for reasons she does not know. She rolls the socks back up and stuffs them into the pillowcase.

On Monday, Granny Lin asks her supervisor for a half day off and takes the bus to the city, looking for socks with the same patterns as the missing ones. She buys several more packs of girls' socks in different designs.

Granny Lin becomes more careful with the laundry now. She makes sure all the girls' socks are in their bags before Kang arrives. From time to time, she scatters around socks that she has bought, all of them having been washed and dried and then rubbed across the floor.

They are still the happy couple on weekends, but Granny Lin worries as she counts the missing socks that she has put out for Kang. She wonders if she needs to talk to him and find out the reason for what he is doing. But every time she opens her mouth she loses her resolve.

On weekends, as they sit in the shadow of the wisteria, Granny Lin wonders if this is the love she missed in her younger years, hand in hand with a dear boy, not asking him to tell her the secret she is not allowed to know.

THE WEATHER GETS hot, and the dorm mothers put mosquito nets over the students' beds. The first night, a boy in the bed next to Kang's gets up after the dorm mother leaves. With a small flashlight in hand, he sticks his head into Kang's mosquito net and shrieks in a low voice, letting the flashlight shine in Kang's eyes. Kang does not cry, as the boy hopes, but the boy is surprised and pleased to find Kang stroking his own cheeks with both his hands in floral socks.

Dorm mothers are called. Seven more socks are discovered, and by the end of the next day everyone in the school knows about the sick boy who steals girls' socks and does strange things with them.

Granny Lin watches the kids chase Kang around the school yard, calling him "sicko," "psycho," "porn boy," her heart wrenching as if it were a piece of rag in the washing machine. Kang is no longer allowed to visit the laundry room. She counts the days to the weekend and is afraid that she will break down before the three days pass.

On Friday afternoon, as they stand in front of the school gate, Granny Lin has to raise Kang's hand up and wave for him. When the shuttle bus is gone, Granny Lin turns to Kang, who is kicking a pebble in front of him.

"Kang, come to Granny's room for a moment," Granny Lin says.

"No, I don't want to," Kang says, letting go of Granny Lin's hand.

"What do you want to do? Let's take a walk."

"I don't want to take a walk."

"How about reading some books? A new case of books came in yesterday."

"I don't want to read."

"Let's get up on the swing."

"I don't want to do anything," Kang says, pushing Granny Lin's hand away from his shoulder.

Granny Lin's tears swell out of her eyes. She looks down at the top of Kang's head. To love someone is to want to please him, even when one is not able to. "Think of something you want to do, and we'll do it together. Think of something you want, and Granny will get it for you. You know Granny loves you."

"I want to go home. I want to see my mom," Kang says. "Granny, do you think we can catch the train and go home for two days?"

Granny Lin looks down at Kang's upturned face, seeing the small hope grow bigger in his eyes. Kang grabs her hand. "Granny, just two days. Nobody will know."

Granny Lin sighs. "Forgive me, Kang. But Granny cannot do this for you."

"But why? You said you'd do anything."

"Anything that we can do here, in the school, in the mountains. Kang, good boy, we cannot leave the school."

It takes a minute for Kang to burst into tears. Granny Lin tries to quiet him and pull him into her arms. Kang pushes her away, and his eyes, with the cold anger that Granny Lin once saw in Old Tang's eyes, chill her. Kang runs across the school yard. Granny Lin runs after him, but has to stop and catch her breath after a few steps. Her old body is failing her young heart.

GRANNY LIN THOUGHT that Kang would be crying in his bed, but the boy is not there. She calls out his name as she walks in the building, checking each unlocked door, the activity room, the music room, the dining hall. She looks under tables and behind curtains, and her heart sinks deeper each time her hope proves unfounded.

For an hour Granny Lin searches, until it occurs to her that the boy may have left the building, and even the school. Paralyzed by such a thought, and imagining all kinds of disasters, she calls the two guards, who are playing poker in the

small room by the schoo.
possibility that the boy has s
insisting that the boy must be
building. More searches are carrie 'o admit the
them. When nothing is yielded, they eac te, both
different worries. the
The police are called. The school supervi. f
The dorm mothers are called. The guards make p.
to whomever they can think of. Granny Lin watches
the young men punch the number with a shaking hand, a.
wonders why he is so nervous. The guards are only losing a
peaceful weekend. They will lose at most a month's salary, as
both are relatives of the trustees. Boys disappear every day—
what would they remember of Kang a year from now even if
they never found him again? Granny Lin begins to cry.

But Kang shows up by himself, in the middle of the tur-
moil, unharmed, hungry, and sleepy. He must have played
hide-and-seek with Granny Lin while she was looking for
him. Or did he want to punish her for disappointing him?
Granny Lin does not know. All she knows is what he told the
school supervisor, that he fell asleep under the piano.

Granny Lin remembers looking under the piano, but nobody trusts an old woman's memory. Besides, what's the difference even if she is telling the truth? She has proved
herself incapable. More stories are remembered—of her eating the students' ration, of her carelessness with the laundry.

On the evening of the day the children return, Granny
Lin is asked to leave. Her things are packed and placed at
the gate: a duffel bag, not heavy even for an old woman.

"The happiness of love is a shooting meteor; the pain of
love is the darkness following." A girl is singing to herself in
a clear voice as she walks past Granny Lin in the street. She

ne girl; the girl moves too fast, and so
ny Lin puts the duffel bag on the ground
breath, still hanging on to the stainless steel
ith her other hand. All the people in the street
know where their legs are taking them. She wonders
when she stopped being one of them.

Someone runs past Granny Lin and pushes her hard on
the back. She stumbles and catches a glimpse of a hand before falling down; a man in a black shirt runs into the crowd
with her duffel bag.

A woman stops and asks, "Are you all right, Granny?"

Granny Lin nods, struggling to recover from the fall. The
woman shakes her head and says aloud to the passersby,
"What a world! Someone just robbed an old granny."

Few people respond; the woman shakes her head again
and moves on.

Granny Lin sits on the street and hugs the lunch pail to
herself. Hungry as people are, it is strange that nobody ever
thinks of robbing an old woman of her lunch. That's why she
has never lost anything important. The three thousand yuan
of dismissal compensation is safe in the lunch pail, as are
several unopened packages of socks, colorful with floral patterns, souvenirs of her brief love story.

After a Life

MR. AND MRS. SU ARE FINISHING BREAKFAST when the telephone rings. Neither moves to pick it up at first. Not many people know their number; fewer use it. Their son, Jian, a sophomore in college now, calls them once a month to report his well-being. He spends most of his holidays and school breaks with his friends' families, not offering even the most superficial excuses. Mr. and Mrs. Su do not have the heart to complain and remind Jian of their wish to see him more often. Their two-bedroom flat, small and cramped as it is, is filled with Beibei's screaming when she is not napping, and a foul smell when she dirties the cloth sheets beneath her. Jian grew up sleeping in a cot in the foyer and hiding from his friends the existence of an elder sister born with severe mental retardation and cerebral palsy. Mr. and Mrs. Su sensed their son's elation when he finally moved into his college dorm. They have held on to the secret wish that after Beibei dies—she is not destined for longevity, after all—they will reclaim their lost son, though neither says anything to the other, both ashamed by the mere thought of the wish.

The ringing stops for a short moment and starts again.

Mr. Su walks to the telephone and puts a hand on the receiver. "Do you want to take it?" he asks his wife.

"So early it must be Mr. Fong," Mrs. Su says.

"Mr. Fong is a man of courtesy. He won't disturb other people's breakfast," Mr. Su says. Still, he picks up the receiver, and his expression relaxes. "Ah, yes, Mrs. Fong. My wife, she is right here," he says, and signals to Mrs. Su.

Mrs. Su does not take the call immediately. She goes into Beibei's bedroom and checks on her, even though it is not time for her to wake up yet. Mrs. Su strokes the hair, light brown and baby-soft, on Beibei's forehead. Beibei is twenty-eight going on twenty-nine; she is so large it takes both her parents to turn her over and clean her; she screams for hours when she is awake, but for Mrs. Su, it takes a wisp of hair to forget all the imperfections.

When she returns to the living room, her husband is still holding the receiver for her, one hand covering the mouthpiece. "She's in a bad mood," he whispers.

Mrs. Su sighs and takes the receiver. "Yes, Mrs. Fong, how are you today?"

"As bad as it can be. My legs are killing me. Listen, my husband just left. He said he was meeting your husband for breakfast and they were going to the stockbrokerage afterward. Tell me it was a lie."

Mrs. Su watches her husband go into Beibei's bedroom. He sits with Beibei often; she does, too, though never at the same time as he does. "My husband is putting on his jacket so he must be going out to meet Mr. Fong now," Mrs. Su says. "Do you want me to check with him?"

"Ask him," Mrs. Fong says.

Mrs. Su walks to Beibei's room and stops at the door. Her husband is sitting on the chair by the bed, his eyes closed for a quick rest. It's eight o'clock, early still, but for an aging man, morning, like everything else, means less than it used to. Mrs. Su goes back to the telephone and says, "Mrs. Fong? Yes, my husband is meeting your husband for breakfast."

"Are you sure? Do me a favor. Follow him and see if he's lying to you. You can never trust men."

Mrs. Su hesitates, and says, "But I'm busy."

"What are you busy with? Listen, my legs are hurting me. I would've gone after him myself otherwise."

"I don't think it looks good for husbands to be followed," Mrs. Su says.

"If your husband goes out every morning and comes home with another woman's scent, why should you care about what looks good or bad?"

It is not her husband who is having an affair, Mrs. Su retorts in her mind, but she doesn't want to point out the illogic. Her husband is indeed often used as a cover for Mr. Fong's affair, and Mrs. Su feels guilty toward Mrs. Fong. "Mrs. Fong, I would help on another day, but today is bad."

"Whatever you say."

"I'm sorry," Mrs. Su says.

Mrs. Fong complains for another minute, of the untrustworthiness of husbands and friends in general, and hangs up. Mrs. Su knocks on the door of Beibei's room and her husband jerks awake, quickly wiping the corner of his mouth. "Mrs. Fong wanted to know if you were meeting Mr. Fong," she says.

"Tell her yes."

"I did."

Mr. Su nods and tucks the blanket tight beneath Beibei's soft, shapeless chin. It bothers Mrs. Su when her husband touches Beibei for any reason, but it must be ridiculous for her to think so. Being jealous of a daughter who understands nothing and a husband who loves the daughter despite that! She will become a crazier woman than Mrs. Fong if she doesn't watch out for her sanity, Mrs. Su thinks, but still, seeing her husband smooth Beibei's hair or rub her cheeks upsets Mrs. Su. She goes back to the kitchen and washes the dishes while her husband gets ready to leave. When he says farewell, she answers politely without turning to look at him.

AT EIGHT-THIRTY Mr. Su leaves the apartment, right on time for the half-hour walk to the stockbrokerage. Most of the time he is there only to study the market; sometimes he buys and sells, executing the transactions with extraordinary prudence, as the money in his account does not belong to him. Mr. Fong has offered the ten thousand yuan as a loan, and has made it clear many times that he is not in any urgent need of the money. It is not a big sum at all for Mr. Fong, a retired senior officer from a military factory, but Mr. Su believes that *for each drop of water one received, one has to repay with a well*. The market and the economy haven't helped him much in returning Mr. Fong's generosity. Mr. Su, however, is not discouraged. A retired mathematics teacher at sixty-five, Mr. Su believes in exercising one's body and mind—both provided by his daily trip to the stockbrokerage—and being patient.

Mr. Su met Mr. Fong a year ago at the stockbrokerage. Mr. Fong, a year senior to Mr. Su, took a seat by him, and conversation started between the two men. He was there out of curiosity, Mr. Fong said; he asked Mr. Su if indeed the stock system would work for the country, and if that was the case, how Marxist political economics could be adapted for this new, clearly capitalistic situation. Mr. Fong's question, obsolete and naive as it was, moved Mr. Su. With almost everyone in the country going crazy about money, and money alone, it was rare to meet someone who was nostalgic about the old but also earnest in his effort to understand the new. "You are on the wrong floor to ask the question," Mr. Su replied. "Those who would make a difference are in the VIP lounges upstairs."

The stockbrokerage, like most of the brokerage firms in Beijing, rented space from bankrupted state-run factories. The one Mr. Su visited used to manufacture color TVs, a profitable factory until it lost a price war to a monopolizing corporation. The laid-off workers were among the ones who frequented the ground floor of the brokerage, opening accounts with their limited means and hoping for good luck. Others on the floor were retirees, men and women of Mr. Su's age who dreamed of making their money grow instead of letting the money die in banks, which offered very low interest rates.

"What are these people doing here if they don't matter to the economy?" Mr. Fong asked.

"*Thousands of sand grains make a tower,*" Mr. Su said. "Together their investments help a lot of factories run."

"But will they make money from the stock market?"

Mr. Su shook his head. He lowered his voice and said, "Most of them don't. Look at that woman there in the first row, the one with the hairnet. She buys and sells according to what the newspapers and television say. She'll never earn money that way. And there, the old man—eighty-two he is, a very fun and healthy oldster but not a wise investor."

Mr. Fong looked at the people Mr. Su pointed out, every one an example of bad investing. "And you, are you making money?" Mr. Fong asked.

"I'm the worst of all," Mr. Su said with a smile. "I don't even have money to get started." Mr. Su had been observing the market for some time. With an imaginary fund, he had practiced trading, dutifully writing down all the transactions in a notebook; he had bought secondhand books on trading and developed his own theories. His prospects of earning money from the market were not bleak at all, he concluded after a year of practice. His pension, however, was small. With a son going to college, a wife and a daughter totally dependent on him, he had not the courage to risk a penny on his personal hobby.

Very quickly, Mr. Fong and Mr. Su became close friends. They sat at teahouses or restaurants, exchanging opinions about the world, from prehistorical times to present day. They were eager to back up each other's views, and at the first sign of disagreement, they changed topics. It surprised Mr. Su that he would make a friend at his age. He was a quiet and lonely man all his life, and most people he knew in his adult life were mere acquaintances. But perhaps this was what made old age a second childhood—friendship came out of companionship easily, with less self-interest, fewer social judgments.

After a month or so, at dinner, Mr. Fong confessed to Mr. Su that he was in a painful situation. Mr. Su poured a cup of rice wine for Mr. Fong, waiting for him to continue.

"I fell in love with this woman I met at a street dance party," Mr. Fong said.

Mr. Su nodded. Mr. Fong had once told him about attending a class to learn ballroom dancing, and had discussed the advantages: good exercise, a great chance to meet people when they were in a pleasant mood, and an aesthetic experience. Mr. Su had thought of teasing Mr. Fong about his surrendering to Western influences, but seeing Mr. Fong's sincerity, Mr. Su had given up the idea.

"The problem is, she is a younger woman," Mr. Fong said.

"How much younger?" Mr. Su asked.

"In her early forties."

"Age should not be a barrier to happiness," Mr. Su said.

"But it's not quite possible."

"Why, is she married?"

"Divorced," Mr. Fong said. "But think about it. She's my daughter's age."

Mr. Su looked Mr. Fong up and down. A soldier all his life, Mr. Fong was in good shape; except for his balding head, he looked younger than his age. "Put on a wig and people will think you are fifty," Mr. Su said. "Quite a decent bridegroom, no?"

"Old Su, don't make fun of me," Mr. Fong said, not concealing a smile. It vanished right away. "It's a futile love, I know."

"Chairman Mao said, *One can achieve anything as long as he dares to imagine it.*"

Mr. Fong shook his head and sullenly sipped his wine. Mr. Su looked at his friend, distressed by love. He downed a cup of wine and felt he was back in his teenage years, consulting his best friend about girls, being consulted. "You know something?" he said. "My wife and I are first cousins. Everybody opposed the marriage, but we got married anyway. You just do it."

"That's quite a courageous thing," Mr. Fong said. "No

wonder I've always had the feeling that you're not an ordinary person. You have to introduce me to your wife. Why don't I come to visit you tomorrow at your home? I need to pay respect to her."

Mr. Su felt a pang of panic. He had not invited a guest to his flat for decades. "Please don't trouble yourself," he said finally. "A wife is just the same old woman after a lifelong marriage, no?" It was a bad joke, and he regretted it right away.

Mr. Fong sighed. "You've got it right, Old Su. But the thing is, a wife is a wife and you can't ditch her like a worn shirt after a life."

It was the first time Mr. Fong mentioned a wife. Mr. Su had thought Mr. Fong a widower, the way he talked only about his children and their families. "You mean, your wife's well and"—Mr. Su thought carefully and said—"she still lives with you?"

"She's in prison," Mr. Fong said and sighed again. He went on to tell the story of his wife. She had been the Party secretary of an import-export branch for the Agriculture Department, and naturally, there had been money coming from subdivisions and companies that needed her approval on paperwork. The usual cash-for-signature transactions, Mr. Fong explained, but someone told on her. She received a *within-the-Party* disciplinary reprimand and was retired. "Fair enough, no? She's never harmed a soul in her life," Mr. Fong said. But unfortunately, right at the time of her retirement, the president issued an order that for corrupt officials who had taken more than a hundred and seventy thousand yuan, the government would seek heavy punishments. "A hundred and seventy thousand is nothing compared to what he's taken!" Mr. Fong hit the table with a fist. In a lower voice, he said, "Believe me, Old Su, only the smaller fish pay

for the government's face-lift. The big ones—they just become bigger and fatter."

Mr. Su nodded. A hundred and seventy thousand yuan
was more than he could imagine, but Mr. Fong must be
right that it was not a horrific crime. "So she had a case with
that number?"

"Right over the limit, and she got a sentence of seven
years."

"Seven years!" Mr. Su said. "How awful and unfair."

Mr. Fong shook his head. "In a word, Old Su, how can I
abandon her now?"

"No," Mr. Su said. "That's not right."

They were silent for a moment, and both drank wine as
they pondered the dilemma. After a while, Mr. Fong said,
"I've been thinking: before my wife comes home, we—the
woman I love and I—maybe we can have a temporary family. No contract, no obligation. Better than those, you know
what they call, one night of something?"

"One-night stands?" Mr. Su blurted out, and then was
embarrassed to have shown familiarity with such improper,
modern vocabularies. He had learned the term from tabloids
the women brought to the brokerage; he had even paid attention to those tales, though he would never admit it.

"Yes. I thought ours could be better than that. *A dew
marriage before the sunrise.*"

"What will happen when your wife comes back?" Mr. Su
asked.

"Seven years is a long time," Mr. Fong said. "Who knows
what will become of me in seven years? I may be resting with
Marx and Engels in heaven then."

"Don't say that, Mr. Fong," Mr. Su said, saddened by the
eventual parting that they could not avoid.

"You're a good friend, Old Su. Thank you for listening to me. All the other people we were friends with—they left us right after my wife's sentence, as if our bad luck would contaminate them. Some of them used to come to our door and beg to entertain us!" Mr. Su said, and then, out of the blue, he brought out the suggestion of loaning Mr. Su some money for investing.

"Definitely not!" Mr. Su said. "I'm your friend not because of your money."

"Ah, how can you think of it that way?" Mr. Fong said. "Let's look at it this way: it's a good experiment for an old Marxist like me. If you make a profit, great; if not, good for my belief, no?"

Mr. Su thought Mr. Fong was drunk, but a few days later, Mr. Fong mentioned the loan again, and Mr. Su found it hard to reject the offer.

MRS. FONG CALLS again two hours later. "I have a great idea," she says when Mrs. Su picks up the phone. "I'll hire a private detective to find out whom my husband is seeing."

"Private detective?"

"Why? You think I can't find the woman? Let me be honest with you—I don't trust that husband of yours at all. I think he lies to you about my husband's whereabouts."

Mrs. Su panics. She didn't know there were private detectives available. It sounds foreign and dangerous. She wonders if they could do some harm to her husband, his being Mr. Fong's accomplice in the affair. "Are you sure you'll find a reliable person?" she says.

"People will do anything if you have the money. Wait till I get the solid evidence," Mrs. Fong says. "The reason I'm calling you is this: if your husband, like you said, is spending every day away from home, wouldn't you be suspicious? Don't you think it possible that they are both having affairs, and are covering up for each other?"

"No, it's impossible."

"How can you be so sure? I'll hire a private detective for both of us if you like."

"Ah, please no," Mrs. Su says.

"You don't have to pay."

"I trust my husband," Mrs. Su says, her legs weakened by sudden fear. Of all the people in the world, a private detective will certainly be the one to find out about Beibei.

"Fine," Mrs. Fong says. "If you say so, I'll spare you the truth."

Mrs. Su has never met Mrs. Fong, who was recently released from prison because of health problems after serving a year of her sentence. A few days into her parole, she called Su's number—it being the only unfamiliar number in Mr. Fong's list of contacts—and grilled Mrs. Su about her relationship with Mr. Fong. Mrs. Su tried her best to convince Mrs. Fong that she had nothing to do with Mr. Fong, nor was there a younger suspect in her household—their only child was a son, Mrs. Su lied. Since then, Mrs. Fong has made Mrs. Su a confidante, calling her several times a day. Life must be hard for Mrs. Fong now, with a criminal record, all her old friends turning their backs on her, and a husband in love with a younger woman. Mrs. Su was not particularly sympathetic with Mrs. Fong when she first learned of the sentence—one hundred and seventy thousand yuan was an astronomical number to her—but now she does not have the heart to refuse Mrs. Fong's friendship. Her husband is surely having a secret affair, Mrs. Fong confesses to Mrs. Su over the phone. He has developed some alarming and annoying habits—flossing his teeth after every meal, doing sit-ups at night, tucking his shirts in more carefully, rubbing hair-growing ointment on his head. "As if he has another forty years to live," Mrs. Fong says. He goes out and meets Mr. Su every day, but what good reason is there for two men to see each other so often?

The stock market, Mrs. Su explains unconvincingly. Mrs. Fong's calls exhaust Mrs. Su, but sometimes, after a quiet morning, she feels anxious for the phone to ring.

Mrs. Su has lived most of her married life within the apartment walls, caring for her children and waiting for them to leave in one way or another. Beyond everyday greetings, she does not talk much with the neighbors when she goes out for groceries. When Mr. and Mrs. Su first moved in, the neighbors tried to pry information from her with questions about the source of all the noises from the apartment. Mrs. Su refused to satisfy their curiosity, and in turn, they were enraged by the denial of their right to know Su's secret. Once when Jian was four or five, a few women trapped him in the building entrance and grilled him for answers; later Mrs. Su found him on the stairs in tears, his lips tightly shut.

Mrs. Su walks to Beibei's bedroom door, which she shut tightly so that Mrs. Fong would not hear Beibei. She listens for a moment to Beibei's screaming before she enters the room. Beibei is behaving quite agitatedly today, the noises she makes shriller and more impatient. Mrs. Su sits by the bed and strokes Beibei's eyebrows; it fails to soothe her into her usual whimpering self. Mrs. Su tries to feed Beibei a few spoonfuls of gruel, but she sputters it all out onto Mrs. Su's face.

Mrs. Su gets up for a towel to clean them both. The

thought of a private detective frightens her. She imagines a
ghostlike man tagging along after Mr. Fong and recording
his daily activities. Would the detective also investigate her
own husband if Mrs. Fong, out of curiosity or boredom,
spends a little more money to find out other people's se-
crets? Mrs. Su shudders. She looks around the bedroom and
wonders if a private detective, despite the curtains and the
window that are kept closed day and night, will be able to
see Beibei through a crack in the wall. Mrs. Su studies
Beibei and imagines how she looks to a stranger: a mountain
of flesh that has never seen the sunshine, white like porcelain. Age has left no mark on Beibei's body and face; she is
still a newborn, soft and tender, wrapped up in an oversized
pink robe.

Beibei screeches and the flesh on her cheeks trembles.
Mrs. Su cups Beibei's plump hand in her own and sings in a
whisper, "The little mouse climbs onto the counter. The little mouse drinks the cooking oil. The little mouse gets too
full to move. Meow, meow, the cat is coming and the little
mouse gets caught."

It was Beibei's favorite song, and Mrs. Su believes there is
a reason for that. Beibei was born against the warning of all
the relatives, who had not agreed with the marriage between
the cousins in the first place. At Beibei's birth, the doctors
said that she would probably die before age ten; it would be
a miracle if she lived to twenty. They suggested the couple
give up the newborn as a specimen for the medical college.
She was useless, after all, for any other reason. Mr. and Mrs.
Su shuddered at the image of their baby soaked in a jar of
formaldehyde, and never brought Beibei back to the hospital
after mother and baby were released. Being in love, the couple were undaunted by the calamity. They moved to a differ-

ent district, away from their families and old neighbors, he changing his job, she giving up working altogether to care for Beibei. They did not invite guests to their home; after a while, they stopped having friends. They applauded when Beibei started making sounds to express her need for comfort and company; they watched her grow up into a bigger version of herself. It was a hard life, but their love for each other, and for the daughter, made it the perfect life Mrs. Su had dreamed of since she had fallen in love at twelve, when her cousin, a year older and already a lanky young man, had handed her a book of poems as a present.

The young cousin has become the stooping husband. The perfect life has turned out less so. The year Beibei reached ten—a miracle worth celebrating, by all means— her husband brought up the idea of a second baby. Why? she asked, and he talked about a healthier marriage, a more complete family. She did not understand his reasoning, and she knew, even when Jian was growing in her belly, that they would get a good baby and that it would do nothing to save them from what had been destroyed. They had built a world around Beibei, but her husband decided to turn away from it in search of a family more like other people's. Mrs. Su found it hard to understand, but then, wasn't there an old saying about men always being interested in change, and women in preservation? A woman accepted anything from life and made it the best; a man bargained for the better but also the less perfect.

Mrs. Su sighs, and looks at Beibei's shapeless features. So offensive she must be to other people's eyes that Mrs. Su wishes she could shrink Beibei back to the size that she once carried in her arms into this room; she wishes she could sneak Beibei into the next world without attracting anybody's attention. Beibei screams louder, white foam dripping by the corner of her mouth. Mrs. Su cleans her with a towel, and for a moment, when her hand stops over Beibei's mouth and muffles the cry, Mrs. Su feels a desire to keep the hand there. Three minutes longer and Beibei could be spared all the struggles and humiliations death has in store for every living creature, Mrs. Su thinks, but at the first sign of blushing in Beibei's pale face, she removes the towel. Beibei breathes heavily. It amazes and saddens Mrs. Su that Beibei's life is so tenacious that it has outlived the love that once made it.

WITH ONE FINGER, Mr. Su types in his password—a combination of Beibei's and Jian's birthdays—at a terminal booth. He is still clumsy in his operation of the computer, but people on the floor, aging and slow as most of them are, are patient with one another. The software dutifully produces graphs and numbers, but Mr. Su finds it hard to concentrate today. After a while, he quits to make room for a woman waiting for a booth. He goes back to the seating area and looks for a good chair to take a rest. The brokerage, in the recent years of a downward economy, has slackened in maintenance, and a lot of chairs are missing orange plastic seats. Mr. Su finally finds a good one among homemade cotton cushions, and sits down by a group of old housewives. The women, in their late fifties or early sixties, are the happiest and chattiest people on the floor. Most of them have money locked into stocks that they have no other choice but to keep for now, and perhaps forever; the only reason for them to come every day is companionship. They talk about their children and grandchildren, unbearable in-laws, soap operas from the night before, stories from tabloids that must be discussed and analyzed at length.

Mr. Su watches the rolling numbers on the big screen. The PA is tuned in to a financial radio station, but the host's analysis is drowned by the women's stories. Most of the time, Mr. Su finds them annoyingly noisy, but today he feels tenderness, almost endearment, toward the women. His wife, quiet and pensive, will never become one of these chatty old hens, but he wishes, for a moment, that one of them were his wife, cheered up by the most mundane matters, mindlessly happy.

After taking note of the numbers concerning him, Mr. Su sighs. Despite all the research he had done, his investment does not show any sign more positive than the old women's. Life goes wrong for the same reason that people miscalculate. Husband and wife promise each other a lifelong love that turns out shorter than a life; people buy stocks with good calculations, but they do not take into consideration life's own preference for, despite the laws of probability, the unlikely. Mr. Su fell in love with his wife at thirteen, and she loved him back. What were the odds for first lovers to end up in a family? Against both families' wills, they married each other, and against everybody's warning, they decided to have a baby. Mr. Su, younger and more arrogant then, calculated and concluded that the odds for a problematic baby were very low, so low that fate was almost on their side. Almost, but not quite, and as a blunt and mean joke, Beibei was born with major problems in her brain and spinal cord. It would not be much of a misfortune except when his wife started to hide herself and the baby from the world; Beibei must have reminded his wife every day that their marriage was less legitimate. There's nothing to be ashamed of, Mr. Su thought of telling her, but he did not have the heart. It was he who suggested another baby. To give them a second chance, to save his wife from the unnecessary shame and pain that she had insisted on living with. Secretly he also wished to challenge fate again. The odds of having another calamity were low, very low, he tried to convince his wife; if only they could have a normal baby, and a normal family! The new baby's birth proved his calculation right—Jian was born healthy, and he grew up into a very handsome and bright boy, as if his parents were awarded doubly for what had been taken away the first time—but who would've thought that such a success, instead of making their marriage a happier one, would turn his wife away from him? How arrogant he was to make the same mistake a second time, thinking he could outsmart life. What had survived the birth of Beibei did not survive Jian's birth, as if his wife, against all common wisdom, could share misfortune with him but not happiness. For twenty years, they have avoided arguments carefully; they have been loving parents, dutiful spouses, but something that had made them crazy for each other as young cousins has abandoned them, leaving them in unshareable pain.

A finger taps Mr. Su's shoulder. He opens his eyes and realizes that he has fallen asleep. "I'm sorry," he says to the woman.

"You were snoring," she says with a reproachful smile.

Mr. Su apologizes again. The woman nods and returns to the conversation with her companions. Mr. Su looks at the clock on the screen, too early for lunch still, but he brings out a bag of instant noodles and a mug from his bag anyway, soaking the noodles with boiling water from the drinking stand. The noodles soften and swell. Mr. Su takes a sip of soup and shakes his head. He thinks of going home and talking to his wife, asking her a few questions he has never gathered enough courage to ask, but then decides that things unsaid had better remain so. Life is not much different from the stock market—you invest in a stock and you stick, and are stuck, to the choice, despite all the possibilities of other mistakes.

At noon, the restaurant commissioned by the stockbrokerage delivers the lunch boxes to the VIP lounges, and the traders on the floor heat lunches in the microwave or make instant noodles. Mr. Su, who is always cheered up by the mixed smells of leftovers from other dinner tables, goes into a terminal booth in a hopeful mood. Someday, he thinks, when his wife is freed from taking care of Beibei, he'll ask her to accompany him to the stockbrokerage. He wants her to see other people's lives, full of meaningless but happy trivialities.

Mr. Su leaves the brokerage promptly at five o'clock. Outside the building, he sees Mr. Fong, sitting on the curb and looking up at him like a sad, deserted child.

"Mr. Fong," Mr. Su says. "Are you all right? Why didn't you come in and find me?"

Mr. Fong suggests they go for a drink, and then holds out a hand and lets Mr. Su pull him to his feet. They find a small roadside diner, and Mr. Fong orders a few cold plates and a bottle of strong yam wine. "Don't you sometimes wish a marriage doesn't go as long as our lives last?" Mr. Fong says over the drink.

"Is there anything wrong?" Mr. Su asks.

"Nothing's right with the wife after she's released," Mr. Fong says.

"Are you going to divorce her?"

Mr. Fong downs a cup of wine. "I wish I could," he says and starts to sob. "I wish I didn't love her at all so I could just pack up and leave."

BY LATE AFTERNOON Mrs. Su is convinced that Beibei is having problems. Her eyes, usually clear and empty, glisten with a strange light, as if she is conscious of her pain. Mrs. Su tries in vain to calm her down, and when all the other ways have failed, she takes out a bottle of sleeping pills. She puts two pills into a small porcelain mortar, and then, after a moment of hesitation, adds two more. Over the years she has fed the syrup with the pill powder to Beibei so that the family can have nights for undisturbed sleep.

Calmed by the syrup, Beibei stops screaming for a short moment, and then starts again. Mrs. Su strokes Beibei's forehead and waits for the medicine to take over her limited consciousness. When the telephone rings, Mrs. Su does not move. Later, when it rings for the fifth time, she checks Beibei's eyes, half closed in drowsiness, and then closes the bedroom door before picking up the receiver.

"Why didn't you answer the phone? Are you tired of me, too?" Mrs. Fong says.

Mrs. Su tries to find excuses, but Mrs. Fong, uninterested in any of them, cuts her off. "I know who the woman is now."

"How much did it cost you to find out?"

"Zero. Listen, the husband—shameless old man—he confessed himself."

Mrs. Su feels relieved. "So the worst is over, Mrs. Fong."

"Over? Not at all. Guess what he said to me this afternoon? He asked me if we could all three of us live together in peace. He said it as if he was thinking on my behalf. 'We have plenty of rooms. It doesn't hurt to give her a room and a bed. She is a good woman, she'll take good care of us both.' Taking care of his *thing,* for sure."

Mrs. Su blushes. "Does she want to live with you?"

"Guess what? She's been laid off. Ha ha, not a surprise, right? I'm sure she wants to move in. Free meals. Free bed. Free man. What comes better? Maybe she's even set her eyes on our inheritance. Imagine what the husband suggested? He said I should think of her as a daughter. He said she lost her father at five and did not have a man good to her until she met him. So I said, Is she looking for a husband, or a stepfather? She's *honey-mouthing* him, you see? But the blind man! He even begged me to feel for her pain. Why didn't he ask her to feel for me?"

Something hits the door with a heavy thump, and then the door swings open. Mrs. Su turns and sees an old man leaning on the door, supported by her husband. "Mr. Fong's drunk," her husband whispers to her.

"Are you there?" Mrs. Fong says.

"Ah, yes, Mrs. Fong, something's come up and I have to go."

"Not yet. I haven't finished the story."

Mrs. Su watches the two men stumble into the bathroom. After a moment, she hears the sounds of vomiting and the running of tap water, her husband's low comforting words, Mr. Fong's weeping.

"So I said, Over my dead body, and he cried and begged and said all these ridiculous things about opening one's mind. Many households have two women and one man living in peace now, he said. It's the marriage revolution, he said. Revolution? I said. It's retrogression. You think yourself a good Marxist, I said, but Marx didn't teach you bigamy. Chairman Mao didn't tell you to have a concubine."

Mr. Su helps Mr. Fong lie down on the couch and he closes his eyes. Mrs. Su watches the old man's tear-smeared face twitch in pain. Soon Mrs. Fong's angry words blend with Mr. Fong's snoring.

With Mr. Fong fast asleep, Mr. Su stands up and walks into Beibei's room. One moment later, he comes out and looks at Mrs. Su with a sad and calm expression that makes her heart tremble. She lets go of the receiver with Mrs. Fong's blabbering and walks to Beibei's bedroom. There she finds Beibei resting undisturbed, the signs of pain gone from her face, porcelain white, with a bluish hue. Mrs. Su kneels by the bed and holds Beibei's hand, still plump and soft, in her own. Her husband comes close and strokes her hair, gray and thin now, but his touch, gentle and timid, is the same one from a lifetime ago, when they were children playing in their grandparents' garden, where the pomegranate blossoms, fire-hued and in the shape of bells, kept the bees busy and happy.

Immortality

HIS STORY, AS THE STORY OF EVERY ONE OF us, started long before we were born. For dynasties, our town provided the imperial families their most reliable servants. Eunuchs they are called, though out of reverence we call them Great Papas. None of us is a direct descendant of a Great Papa, but traveling upstream in the river of our blood, we find uncles, brothers, and cousins who gave up their maleness so that our names would not vanish in history. Generations of boys, at the age of seven or eight, were chosen and castrated—*cleaned* as it was called—and sent into the palace as apprentices, learning to perform domestic tasks for the emperor and his family. At the age of thirteen or fourteen, they started to earn their allowances, silver coins that they saved and sent home to their parents. The coins were kept in a trunk, along with a small silk sack in which the severed male root was preserved with herbs. When the brothers of Great Papas reached the marriage age, their parents unlocked the trunk and brought out the silver coins. The money allowed the brothers to marry their wives; the wives gave birth to their sons; the sons grew up to carry on the family name, either by giving birth to more sons or by going into the palace as cleaned boys. Years went by. When Great Papas could no longer serve the imperial masters on their wobbly knees, they were released from the palace and taken in by their nephews. Nothing left for them to worry about, they sat all day in the sun and stroked the cats they had brought home from the palace, fat and slow as they themselves were, and watched the male dogs chasing the females in the alleys. In time death came for them. Their funerals were the most spectacular events in our town: sixty-four Buddhist monks, in gold and red robes, chanted prayers for forty-nine days to lead their souls into the heaven; sixty-four Tao masters, in blue and gray robes, danced for forty-nine days to drive away any evils that dared to attach to their bodies. The divine moment came at the end of the forty-nine days, when the silk sacks containing their withered male roots were placed in the coffins. Now that the missing part had rejoined the body, the soul could leave without regret, to a place better than our town.

This was the story of every one of our Great Papas. For dynasties they were the most trustworthy members of the imperial family. They tended to the princesses' and the concubines' most personal tasks without tainting the noble blood with the low and dirty desires of men; they served the emperor and the princes with delicacy, yet, unlike those young handmaids who dreamed of seducing the emperor and his sons with their cheap beauties, Great Papas posed no threat to the imperial wives. There were wild rumors, though, about them serving as playthings for the princes before they reached the legal age to take concubines, and unfortunate tales of Great Papas being drowned, burned, bludgeoned, beheaded for the smallest mistakes, but such stories, as we all know, were made up to attack the good

name of our town. What we believe is what we have seen—
the exquisitely carved tombstones in our cemetery, the ele-
gantly embroidered portraits in our family books. Great
Papas filled our hearts with pride and gratitude. If not for
them, who were we, the small people born into this no-
name town?

The glory of our town has faded in the past century. But
may I tell you one boy's story before I reach the falling of
Great Papas in history? As a tradition, the boys sent to the
palace were not to be the only sons, who held the even more
sacred duty of siring more boys. But the greatest among our
Great Papas was an only son of his family. His father, also an
only son, died young before he had the chance to plant more
seeds in his wife's belly. With no uncle or brother to send
them money from the palace, the boy and his widowed
mother lived in poverty. At ten years old, after a fight with
the neighbors' boys who had bragged about their brothers
accepting gold bricks from the emperor's hands, the boy
went into the cowshed and cleaned himself, with a rope and
a sickle. According to the legend, the boy walked across the
town, his male root dripping blood in his hand, and shouted
to the people watching on with pity in their eyes, "Wait till I
become the best servant of His Majesty!" Unable to endure
the shame and the despair of living under a sonless and
grandsonless roof, his mother threw herself into a well.
Twenty years later, the son became the master eunuch in
the palace, taking under his charge twenty-eight hundred
eunuchs and thirty-two hundred handmaids. With no brothers to send his money to, he saved every coin and retired as
the richest man in the region. He hired men to dig out his
poor mother's coffin and gave her a second funeral, the most
extravagant one ever to take place in our town. It was in the

ninth month of 1904, and to this day our old people haven't stopped talking about every detail of the funeral: the huge coffin carved out of a sandalwood tree, stacks of gold bricks, trunks of silk clothes, and cases of jade bowls for her to use in the next life. Even more impressive were the four young girls the son had purchased from the poor peasants on the mountain, all of them twelve years old. They were put into satin dresses they would have never dreamed of wearing and were each fed a cup of mercury. The mercury killed them instantly, so their peachy complexions were preserved when they were paraded in sedan chairs before the coffin. With burning incense planted in their curled fingers, the four girls accompanied the mother to the other world as her loyal handmaids.

This Great Papa's story was the brightest page in our history, like that one most splendid firework streaking the sky before darkness floods in. Soon the last dynasty was overthrown by republics. The emperor was driven out of the Forbidden City; so were his most loyal servants, the last generation of our Great Papas. By the 1930s most of them lived in poverty in the temples around the Forbidden City. Only the smartest ones earned a fair living by showing their bodies to Western reporters and tourists, charging extra for answering questions, even more for having their pictures taken.

THEN WE HAVE a short decade of republic, the warlords, two world wars, in both of which we fought on the winning side yet winning nothing, the civil war, and finally we see the dawn of communism. The day the dictator claims the communist victory in our country, a young carpenter in our town comes home to his newly wedded wife.

"It says we are going to have a new life from now on," the

young wife tells the husband, pointing to a loudspeaker on their roof.

"New or old, life is the same," the husband replies. He gets his wife into bed and makes love to her, his eyes half closed in ecstasy while the loudspeaker is broadcasting a new song, with men and women repeating the same lyrics over and over.

This is how the son is conceived, in a chorus of *Communism is so great, so great, and so great.* The same song is broadcast day after day, and the young mother hums along, touching her growing belly, and cutting carefully the dictator's pictures from newspapers. Of course we never call him the dictator. We call him Our Father, Our Savior, the North Star of Our Lives, the Never Falling Sun of Our Era. Like most women of her generation, the mother is illiterate. Yet unlike others, she likes to look at newspapers, and she saves the pictures of the dictator in a thick notebook. Isn't she the woman with the greatest wisdom in our town? No other woman would ever think of watching the dictator's face while pregnant with a son. Of course there has always been the saying that the more a pregnant woman studies a face, the greater the possibility of the baby owning that face. Years ago, young mothers in the cities liked to watch one kind of imported doll, all of them having a foreign name, Shirley Temple. Decades later, movie stars will be the most studied faces among the pregnant mothers. But at this time the dictator is the only superstar in the media, so the mother has been gazing at the dictator's face for ten months before the baby's birth.

The son is born with the dictator's face, a miracle unnoticed by us at first. For the next ten years we will avoid looking at him, for fear we will see his dead father in his face.

The father was a hardworking man, nice to his neighbors, good to his wife. We would have never imagined that he would be an enemy of our newborn communist nation. Yet there are witnesses, not one, but a whole pub of evening drinkers.

What gets him killed is his comment about heroes and sows. At this time, we respect the communist power above us as our big brother. In our big-brother country, the Soviet Union, it is said, women are encouraged to produce babies for the communist cause, and those who have given birth to a certain number of babies are granted the title *mother hero*. Now that we are on the same highway to the same heaven, the dictator decides to adopt the same policy.

The young carpenter is a little drunk when he jokes aloud to his fellow drinkers, "Mother heroes? My sow has given birth to ten babies in a litter. Shouldn't she be granted a title too?"

That's it, a malicious attack on the dictator's population policy. The carpenter is executed after a public trial. All but his wife attend the meeting, every one of us sticking our fists high and hailing the People's victory, our unanimous voice drowning out his wife's moan from her bed. We shout slogans when the bullet hits the young man's head. We chant revolutionary songs when his body is paraded in the street. When we finally lose our voices from exhaustion, we hear the boy's first cry, loud and painful, and for a moment, it is difficult for us to look into one another's eyes. What have we done to a mother and a baby? Wasn't the dead young man one of our brothers?

What we do not know, at the time, is that a scholar in the capital has been thrown in jail and tortured to death for predicting a population explosion and calling for the dictator to change the policy. Nor do we know that in a meeting with the leader of the big-brother country in Moscow, the dictator has said that we do not fear another world war or nuclear weapons: *Let the Americans drop the atomic bombs on our heads. We have five hundred million people in our nation. Even if half of us are killed, we still have two hundred and fifty million, and these two hundred and fifty million would produce another two hundred and fifty million in no time.*

Later, when we read his words in the newspaper, our blood boils. For the years to come, we will live with our eyes turned to the sky, waiting for the American bombs to rain down on us, waiting to prove to the dictator our courage, and our loyalty.

THE BOY GROWS up fast like a bamboo shoot. The mother grows old even faster. After the carpenter's death, upon her request, the Revolution Committee in our town gives her a job as our street sweeper. Every dawn, we lie in our beds and listen to the rustling of her bamboo broom. She has become a widow at the age of eighteen, as beautiful as a young widow could be, and naturally some of our bachelors cannot help but fantasize about her in their single beds. Yet none of our young men offers her another marriage. Who wants to marry a counterrevolutionary's widow and spend the rest of his life worrying about being a sympathizer of the wrong person? What's more, even though the dictator has said that men and women are equal in our nation, we still believe a widow who wants another husband is a whore inside. Our belief is confirmed when we read in newspapers the dictator's comment about one of his close followers who has become an enemy of the nation: *A man cannot conceal his reactionary nature forever, just as a widow cannot hide her desire to be fucked.*

So the young mother withers in our eyes. Her face becomes paler each day, and her eyes drier. By the time the boy is ten, the mother looks like a woman of sixty. None of our bachelors bothers to lay his eyes on her face anymore.

The boy turns ten the year the famine starts. Before the famine, for three years, we have been doing nothing except singing for our communist heaven and vowing to liberate the suffering working class around the world. Farmers and workers have stopped toiling, their days spent in the pains and joys of composing yet another poem, competing to be the most productive proletarian poet. We go to the town center every day to discuss the strategy of how to conquer the world under the leadership of the dictator. When the famine catches us unprepared, we listen to the dictator's encouraging words in the loudspeakers. He calls for us to make our belts one notch tighter for our communist future, and we happily punch more holes in them. The second year of the famine, the dictator says in the loudspeakers: *Get rid of the sparrows and the rats; they are the thieves who stole our food and brought hunger to us.*

Killing sparrows is the most festive event in the three long years of famine. After months of drinking thin porridges and eating weed roots, on the morning of the sparrow-killing day we each get two steamed buns from the municipal dining room. After breakfast we climb to the roof of every house, and start to strike gongs and drums at the Revolution Committee's signal. From roof to roof, our arrhythmic playing drives the sparrows into the sky. All morning and all afternoon we play, in different shifts, and whenever a sparrow tries to rest in a treetop we shoo him away with colorful flags bound to long bamboo poles. In the evening the sparrows start to rain down on us like little bombs, dying in horror and exhaustion. Kids decorated as little scarecrows run around, collecting the dead sparrows for our dinner.

The boy is trying to sneak a sparrow into his sleeve when a bigger boy snatches his hand. "He is stealing the property of the People," the big boy shouts to the town.

"My mom is sick. She needs to eat something," the boy says.

"Hey, boy, what your mom needs is not this kind of bird," a man says, and we roar with laughter. The buns in our stomachs and the sparrows in the baskets have put us in a good mood.

The boy stares at the man for a moment and smacks into him with his head.

"Son of a bitch," the man says, bending over and covering his crotch with his hands.

"Beat the little counterrevolutionary," someone says, and we swarm toward the boy with fists and feet. The famine has made us angrier each day, and we are relieved to have found someone to vent our nameless rage.

The mother rushes into the crowd and tries to push us away. Her presence makes us hit the boy even harder. Some of us pick up bricks and boulders, ready to knock him out. Some of us bare our teeth, ready to eat him alive.

"You all look at his face. Whoever dares to touch him one more time, I'll sue him for his disrespect for our greatest leader," the mother yells, charging at us like a crazy woman.

Our bodies freeze. We look at the boy's face. Even with his swollen face and black eyes, we have no problem telling that he has the face of the dictator, young and rebellious, just as in the illustrations in the books about the dictator's heroic childhood. The boy stands up and limps to his mother. We look at his face in awe, not daring to move when he spits bloody phlegm at our feet.

"Remember this face," the boy says. "You will have to pay for this one day." He picks up a couple of sparrows and walks away with his mother. We watch them supporting each other like husband and wife.

FOR YEARS WE do not know if it is a blessing or a disaster that a boy with the dictator's face lives among us. We treat the boy and his mother as the most precious and fragile treasure we have, never breathing one word about them to an outsider.

"It may not be a good thing," our old people warn us, and tell us the story of one of our Great Papas, who happened to have the same nickname as the emperor and was thrown into a well to drown. "There are things that are not allowed to exist in duplicates," the old people say.

Yet none of us dares to say one disrespectful word about the boy's face. As he grows older, he looks more and more like the dictator. Sometimes as we walk past him in the street, there is a surge of warmth in our chests, as if the dictator himself were with us. This is the time when the dictator becomes larger than the universe in our nation. Illiterate housewives who have used old newspapers as wallpaper and who have, accidentally, reversed the titles with the dictator's name in them are executed. Parents of little first-graders who have misspelled the dictator's name are sent to labor camps. With the boy living among us, we are constantly walking on a thin layer of ice above deep water. We worry about not paying enough respect to the face, an indication of our hidden hatred of the dictator. We worry about respecting that face too much, which could be interpreted as our inability to tell the false from the true, worshipping the wrong idol. In our school the teachers never speak one harsh word to him. Whatever games the students play, the side without him is willing to lose. When he graduates from the high school, the Revolution Committee has meetings for weeks to discuss what is an appropriate job for a young man with a face like his. None of the jobs we have in town is safe enough to be given to him. Finally we think we have come up with the best solution to the problem—we elect him as the director of the advisory board to the Revolution Committee.

The young man prospers. Having nothing to do, and not liking to kill his time over cups of tea with the old board members, he walks around town every day, talking to people who are flattered by his greetings, and watching the female sales assistants in the department store blush at his sight. His mother is in much better shape now, with more color in her face. The only inconvenience is that no girl will date the young man. We have warned our daughters that marrying him would either be the greatest fortune or the greatest misfortune. Born into a town where gambling is genuinely disapproved of, none of us wants to marry a daughter off to a man like him.

THE DAY THE dictator dies, we gather at the town center and cry like orphans. On the only television set our town owns, we watch the whole nation howling with us. For three months we wear black mourning armbands to work and to sleep. All entertainments are banned for six months. Even a year or two after his death, we still look sideways at those women who are growing bellies, knowing that they have been insincere in their mourning. Fathers of those children never receive respect from us again.

It is a difficult time for the young man. Upon seeing his face, some of us break into uncontrollable wails, and he himself has to spend hours crying with us. It must have tired him. For a year he stays in his own room, and the next time we see him, walking toward the town center with a small suitcase, he looks much older than his age of twenty-eight.

"Is there anything wrong?" we greet him with concern. "Don't let too much grief drag you down."

"Thank you, but I am in a fine state," the young man replies.

"Are you leaving for somewhere?"

"Yes, I am leaving."

"Where to?" We feel a pang of panic. Losing him at this time seems as unbearable as losing the dictator one year ago.

"It's a political assignment," the young man says with a mysterious smile. "Classified."

Only after he is driven away in a well-curtained luxury car (the only car most of us have ever seen in our lives) do we catch the news that he is going to the capital for an audition as the dictator's impersonator. It takes us days of discussion among ourselves to figure out what words like "audition" and "impersonator" mean. In the end the only agreement we come to is that he is going to become a great man.

Now that he has disappeared from our sights, his mother becomes the only source for stories of him. A proud mother as she is, every time we inquire of her regarding his whereabouts, she repeats the story of how she gazed at the late dictator's face day and night when her son was growing inside her. "You know, it's like he is the son of our great leader," she says.

"Yes, all of us are sons of our great leader," we nod and say. "But surely he is the best son."

The mother sighs with great satisfaction. She remembers how in the first few years after her son was born, women of her age produced baby after baby, putting framed certificates of mother heroes on their walls and walking past her with their eyes turning to the sky. Let time prove who is the real hero, she would think and smile to herself.

Then she tells us about her son, every bit of information opening a new door to the world. He rode in the first-class car in a train to the capital, where he and other candidates have settled down in a luxury hotel, and are taken to the dictator's memorial museum every day, studying for the competition.

"Are there other candidates?" we gasp, shocked that she may not be the only woman to have studied the dictator's face during pregnancy.

"I am sure he is the one they want," the mother says. "He says he has total confidence, when he looks at the leader's face, that he is going to be the chosen one."

In the years to come, some among us will have the chance to go to the capital and wait in a long line for hours to take a look at the dictator's face. After his death, a memorial museum was built in the center of our nation's capital, and the dictator's body is kept there in a crystal coffin. *Let our great leader live for ten thousand years in the hearts of a hundred generations* is what the designer has carved into the entrance of the museum. Inside the entrance we will pay a substantial fee for a white paper flower to be placed at the foot of the crystal coffin, among a sea of white flowers. For a brief moment, some of us will wonder whether the flowers are collected from the base and resold the next day, but instantly we will feel ashamed of ourselves for thinking such impure thoughts in the most sacred place in the world. With the flowers in hand we will walk into the heart of the memorial, in a single hushed file, and we will see the dictator, lying in the transparent coffin, covered by a huge red flag decorated with golden stars, his eyes closed as if in sleep, his mouth in a smile. We will be so impressed with this great man's body that we will ignore the unnatural red color in his cheeks, and his swollen neck as thick as his head.

Our young man must have walked the same route and looked at his face with the same reverence. What else has passed through his heart that does not occur to us? we will wonder.

He must have felt closer to the great man than any one of us. He has the right to feel so, chosen among tens of candidates as the dictator's impersonator. How he beat his rivals his mother never tells us in detail, just saying that he was born for the role. Only much later do we hear the story: our young man and the other candidates spend days in training, and those who are too short or too weak-built for the dictator's stature (even they, too, have the dictator's face) are eliminated in the first round, followed by those who cannot master the dictator's accent. Then there are the candidates who have everything except a clean personal history, like those born to the landlord class. Thanks to the Revolution Committee in our town, which has concealed the history of our young man being the son of an executed counterrevolutionary, he makes it into the final round with three other men. On the final day, when asked to do an improvised performance, the other three candidates all choose to quote the dictator announcing the birth of our communist nation (which is, as you remember, also the beginning of our young man's own journey), while he, for reasons unknown, says, "*A man cannot conceal his reactionary nature forever, just as a widow cannot hide her desire to be fucked.*"

For a moment, he is horrified by his blunder, and feels the same shame and anger he once felt as a dead sparrow turned cold between his fingers. To his surprise, he is chosen, the reason being that he has caught the essence of the dictator, while the other three only got the rough shape. The three of them are sent with the rest of the candidates for plastic surgery, for, as our old men have said, there are things that are not allowed to exist in duplicate.

OUR YOUNG MAN becomes the sole face that represents the dictator in the nation, and thus start the most glorious years of his life. Movies about the dictator, starring our young man, are filmed by the government-run movie factories. Back in town, we cram into our only theater and watch the movies, secretly blaming our mothers or wives for not having given birth to a great face.

The marriage of the young man becomes our biggest concern. He is over thirty now, an age generally considered indecent for our young daughters. But who will care about the age of a great man? The old-style ones among us hire matchmakers for our daughters, and send with them expensive gifts to his mother. Others, more modern and aggressive, knock on his mother's door with blushing daughters trailing behind. Dazed by the choices, his mother goes to the town center and makes long-distance calls to him every other day, reporting yet another suitable candidate. But he is no longer a man of our town. He has been flying all over the nation for celebrations and movies; he has seen more attractive women than our town can provide. Through his apologetic mother, he rejects all of our offers. Accepting that our town is too shallow a basin to contain a real dragon, most of us give up and marry our daughters off to local young men. Yet some among us cling to the nonexistent hope, waiting for the day when he will realize the incomparable beauty and virtue of our daughters. For a number of years, scores of girls in our town are kept untouched by their parents. Too much looking forward makes their necks grow longer each year. It is not an unfamiliar sight to see a girl with a crane-like neck walk past us in the street, guarded by her parents, who have grown to resemble giraffes.

The young man is too occupied with his new role to know such stories. He appears in the national celebrations for all the holidays. His most loyal audience, we sit all night long in front of the television and wait for his appearance. On the screen, men and women sing and dance with hearty smiles on their faces like well-trained kindergarteners. Children four or five years old flirt with one another, singing love songs like joyful parrots. At such moments, those of us who think a little more than others start to feel uneasy, haunted by a strange fear that our people are growing down, instead of growing up. But the worry vanishes when our young man, the dictator's impersonator, shows up. People on the screen stand up in ovation and hold out their hands to be shaken. Young women with the prettiest faces rush to him with bouquets of flowers. Kids swarm around him and call him by the name of the dictator. Nostalgic tears fill everyone's eyes. For a moment we believe time has stopped. The dictator is still alive among us, and we are happily living as his sons.

BUT TIME HAS sneaked by while we were mesmerized by our young man's face. Now we have Sony and Panasonic; we have Procter & Gamble, Johnson & Johnson. We have imported movies in which men and women hold hands freely in the street, and they even kiss each other without a trace of fear in their eyes. Our life, we realize, is not as happy as we have been taught to think. People in those capitalist countries are not waiting for us to be their liberators. They never know of our love for them.

This must be a difficult period for our young man as well. Biographies and memoirs about the dictator appear overnight like spring grass. Unlike the books written collectively by the government-assigned writing groups, these books spell trouble the moment they appear. Soon they are decided to be illegal publications, and are confiscated and burned in great piles. Yet some of the words have spread out, bad words about the dictator. Mouth to mouth the rumors travel, how under his reign fifty million people have died from famine and political persecution. But if you looked at the number closely, you would realize it is far less than what the dictator was once willing to sacrifice to American nuclear bombs. So what is all the fuss about?

Still, we start to think about what we have been led to believe all these years. Once doubt starts, it runs rampant in our hearts like wildfire. Our young man's face appears on the television regularly, but the face has lost its aura. Those of us who have been waiting for his proposal are eager to sell our daughters to the first offer available. The young man's mother, now a garrulous old woman, walks in the street and grabs whomever she can to tell his stories, none of which impresses us anymore. From his mother we have learned that he is touring across the nation with our present leader, a trip designed to inspire our national belief in communism. So what? we ask, and walk away before the mother has the chance to elaborate.

The tour ends early when a protest breaks out in the capital. Thousands of people rally for democracy in the center of the capital, where the dictator's memorial museum is less and less visited. Threatened and infuriated, our present leader orders the army to fire machine guns at the protesters. Astonishing as the event is, it slips out of our memory as soon as the dead are burned to ashes in the state-supervised crematoriums. The leader has said, as we later read in newspapers, that he is willing to kill two hundred thousand lives in exchange for twenty years of communist stability. Numbed by such numbers, we will echo his words and applaud his wisdom when we are required to publicly condemn those killed in the incident.

In no time the big-brother country above us no longer exists. Then one by one our comrades in arms take turns exiting the historical stage. Confused as we are, we do not know what to think of them, whether we should envy, despise, or pity them.

LIFE IS PRESENTING a big problem to our young man at this time. Although out of habit we still call him our young man, he is no longer young but in his forties. Even worse, he is a man in his forties who has never tasted a woman in his life. Can you believe it? we will ask one another after all that is to come. Incredible; we will shake our heads. But it is true: our young man spent most of his twenties wanting a woman but we were unwilling to hand our daughters to him; when we were ready, he had become a man too great for our daughters. Time passes ruthlessly. Now that none of our daughters is available anymore, he starts to fantasize about the women he should have had long ago.

Once the desire is awakened, he is no longer able to live in peace. He watches women walking in the streets, their bare arms and legs in summer dresses deliciously attractive, and wonders how it would feel to have a woman of his own. Yet which woman is worthy of his greatness? Sometimes his blood is so unruly that he feels the urge to grab anyone passing by and make her his woman. But once his desire is subdued, after successful masturbation, he is no longer driven by blind craving. At such moments he sees his life more clearly than ever, and he knows that no woman is great enough to match him.

"But you need a wife to give birth to a son," his mother, eager for a grandson, reminds him when he calls long distance to speak to her. "Remember, the first and the foremost duty of a man is to make a son, and pass on his family name."

He mumbles indistinct words and hangs up. He knows that no woman's womb will nurture a son with a face as great as his own.

NOW THAT THE dictator's life has been explored and filmed thoroughly, our young man has more time on his hands. When there is no celebration to attend, he wanders in the street with a heavy coat, his face covered by the high collar and a pair of huge dark glasses. Sometimes he feels the temptation to walk with his face completely bare to the world, but the memory of being surrounded by hundreds of people asking for autographs stops him from taking the risk.

One day he walks across the capital, in search of something he is eager to have but unable to name. When he enters an alley, someone calls to him from behind a cart of newspapers and magazines.

"Want some books, friend?"

He stops and looks at the vendor from behind his dark glasses. "What kind of books?"

"What kind do you want?"

"What kind do you have?"

The vendor moves some magazines and uncovers the plastic sheet beneath the magazines. "Yellows, reds, whatever you want. Fifty yuan a book."

He bends over and looks from above his dark glasses. Underneath the plastic sheet are books with colorful covers. He picks one up and looks at a man and a woman, both naked, copulating in a strange position on the cover. His heart starts to beat in his chest, loud and urgent.

"That's a good yellow one," the vendor says, "as yellow as you want."

He clasps the book with his fingers. "What else do you have?"

"How about this red one?" The vendor hands him another book, the dictator's face on the cover. "Everybody loves this book."

He has heard of the book, a memoir written by the dictator's physician of thirty years, banned when it was published abroad, and smuggled into the country from Hong Kong and America.

He pays for the two books and walks back to his room. He studies the dictator's portrait and compares it with his own face in the mirror, still perfect from every angle. He sighs and plunges into the yellow book, devouring it like a starved man. When his erection becomes too painful, he forces himself to drop the book and pick up the red one.

He feels an emptiness that he has never felt before, switching between the books when one becomes too unbearable. In the yellow book he sees a world he has missed all his life, in which a man has an endless supply of women, all of them eager to please him. Yet for all he knows, the only man who could have as many women as he wants is the dictator. He leafs through the red book one more time, looking at the pictures of the dictator in the company of young attractive *nurses,* and realizes that he has misunderstood his role all these years. To be a great man means to have whatever he wants from the world. Blaming himself for this belated understanding, he stands up and goes out into the night.

He has no difficulty locating a prostitute in the dimly lit karaoke-and-dance bar. As a precaution he keeps his dark glasses and heavy coat on the whole time they are bargaining. Then he goes away with the young woman to a nearby hotel, sneaking through a side door into a room the woman has reserved, while she deals with the receptionist.

What comes next is perplexing to us. All we can figure out from the rumors is that when he is asked to undress, he refuses to take off either his dark glasses or his heavy coat. To be a great man means to have a woman in whatever way he wants, our young man must be thinking. But how is a man like him able to resist the skillful fingers of a professional like the woman he has hired? In a confusing moment, he is as naked as the woman, his face bare and easy to recognize. Before he realizes it, the woman's pimp, dressed up in police uniform, rushes in with a pair of handcuffs and a camera. Lights flash and snapshots are taken, his hands cuffed and clothes confiscated. Only then does the couple recognize his face, and we can imagine how overjoyed they must be by such a discovery. Instead of the usual amount, they ask for ten times what others pay, because our young man is a celebrity and should pay a celebrity price for the pictures.

To this day we still disagree on how our young man should have reacted. Some of us think he should have paid and let himself go free, money being no problem for him. Others think he did nothing wrong by refusing to cooperate, but he should have gone to the police and reported the couple, instead of thinking such things would pass unnoticed. After the night, rumors start to spread across the capital, vivid stories about our young man's regular visits to the illegal brothels. The pictures he has failed to secure are circulated in different circles, until everyone in the capital claims that he has seen them. None of us in town has seen the pictures. Still, our hearts are broken when we imagine his body, naked and helpless, and we try our best to keep our mind's eyes away from the familiar face in those pictures.

He is considered unsuitable to continue as the impersonator of the dictator, for, as it is put in the letter addressed to him by the Central Committee of Cultural Regulation, he has soiled the name he is representing. Never before had it occurred to him that a man like him could be fired. There is no other face like his in the world, and who would replace him, the most irreplaceable man in the nation? He goes from office to office, begging for another chance, vowing never to touch a woman again. What he does not understand is that his role is no longer needed. A new leader has come into power and proclaimed himself the greatest guide of our communist cause in the new millennium. Talent scouts are combing through the nation for a new perfect face different from his own.

So our no longer young man comes home on a gloomy winter day. Stricken by shame, his mother has turned ill overnight and left us before he makes his way back. The day he arrives, some of us—those who remember him as the boy with a sparrow in his hand, who have secretly wished him to be our son-in-law, who have followed his path for years as the loyal audience of his mother, and who have, despite the pain of seeing him fall, lived for the joy of seeing his face— yes, those of us who have been salvaged from our mundane lives by loving him, we gather at the bus stop and hold out our hands for him to shake. He gets off the bus and ignores our earnest smiles, his dark glasses and high collar covering his face. Watching him walk to his mother's grave, with a long shadow limping behind him, we decide we will forgive him for his rudeness. Who would have the heart to blame a son like him? No matter what has happened to him, he is still the greatest man in our history, our boy and our hero.

TRUST US, IT breaks our hearts when he cleans himself by his mother's tomb. How such a thought occurred to him we will never understand, especially since, if we are not mistaken, he is still a virgin who has so much to look forward to in life. The night it happens, we hear a long howl in our sleep. We rush outside into the cold night and find him in our cemetery. Even though we have grown up listening to the legends of our Great Papas, the scene makes us sick to our bones. We wonder what the meaning of such an act is. No one in our town—not we the small people, not our Great Papas—has reached the height that he has. Even our greatest Great Papa was only the best servant of the emperor, while he, with the face of the dictator, was once the emperor himself. Watching him roll over on the ground, his face smeared with tears and blood, we remember the story of the ten-year-old boy, his male root in his hand, his face calm and proud. This is a sad moment for us, knowing that we, the children of our Great Papas, will never live up to their legends.

But lamenting aside, we still have a newly cleaned man to deal with. Some of us insist on sending him to the hospital for emergency treatment; others consider such a move unnecessary, for the act is done and there is no more harm left. Confused as we are, none of us remembers to collect the most important thing at the scene. Later, when we realize our mistake, we spend days searching every inch of our cemetery. Yet the missing part from his body has already disappeared, to whose mouth we do not want to imagine.

He survives, not to our surprise. Hadn't all our Great Papas survived and lived out their heroic stories? He is among us now, with a long barren life ahead. He sits in the sun and watches the dogs chasing one another, his face hidden behind dark glasses and the high collar of his coat. He walks to the cemetery in the dusk and talks to his mother until the night falls.

As for us, we have seen him born in pain and we will, in time, see him die in pain. The only thing we worry about is his next life. With his male root forever missing, what will we put into the silk sack to bury with him? How will we be able to send a soul to the next world in such incompleteness?

For the peace of our own minds, every day we pray for his health. We pray for him to live forever as we prayed for the dictator. He is the man whose story we do not want to end, and as far as we can see, there will be no end to his story.

The Princess of Nebraska

SASHA LOOKED AT BOSHEN IN THE WAITING line for a moment before turning her eyes to the window. She wished that she would never have to see Boshen again after this trip. She had run to the bathroom the moment they entered the McDonald's, leaving him to order for them both. He had suggested a good meal in Chinatown, and she had refused. She wanted to see downtown Chicago before going to the clinic at Planned Parenthood the next morning. It was the only reason for her to ride the Greyhound bus all day from Nebraska. Kansas City would have been a wiser choice, closer, cheaper, but there was nothing to see there—the trip was not meant for sightseeing, but Sasha hoped to get at least something out of it. She did not want to spend all her money only to remember a drugged sleep in a dreary motel in the middle of nowhere. Sasha had grown up in a small town in Inner Mongolia; vast and empty landscapes depressed her.

"You must be tired," Boshen said as he pushed the tray of food to Sasha, who had taken a table by the window. She looked tiny in the oversized sweatshirt. Her face was slightly swollen, and the way she checked out the customers in the

(68)

store, her eyes staying on each face a moment too long, moved him. She was twenty-one, a child still.

"I got a fish sandwich for you," Boshen said when Sasha did not answer him.

"I haven't seen one happy face since arriving," Sasha said. "What's the other one?"

"Chicken."

Sasha threw the fish sandwich across the table and grabbed the chicken sandwich from Boshen's tray. "I hate fish," she said.

"It's good for you now," Boshen said.

"Now will be over soon," Sasha said. She looked forward to the moment when she was ready to move on. "Moving on" was a phrase she just learned, an American concept that suited her well. It was such a wonderful phrase that Sasha could almost see herself stapling her Chinese life, one staple after another around the pages until they became one solid block that nobody would be able to open and read. She would have a fresh page then, for her American life. She was four months late already.

Boshen said nothing and unwrapped the fish sandwich. It was a change—sitting at a table and having an ordered meal—after months of eating in the kitchen of the Chinese restaurant where he worked as a helper to the Sichuan chef. Boshen had come to America via a false marriage to a friend five months earlier, when he had been put under house arrest for his correspondence with a Western reporter regarding a potential AIDS epidemic in a central province. He had had to publish a written confession of his wrongdoing to earn his freedom. A lesbian friend, a newly naturalized American citizen herself, had offered to marry him out of China. Before that, he had lived an openly gay life in Beijing, madly in love with Yang, an eighteen-year-old boy. Boshen had tried different ways to contact Yang since he had arrived in America, but the boy never responded. The checks Boshen sent him were not cashed, either.

They ate without speaking. Sasha swallowed her food fast, and waited for Boshen to finish his. Outside the window, more and more people appeared, all moving toward downtown, red reindeer's antlers on the heads of children who sat astride their fathers' shoulders. Boshen saw the question in Sasha's eyes and told her that there was a parade that evening, and all the trees on Michigan Avenue would light up for the coming Thanksgiving and Christmas holidays. "Do you want to stay for it?" he asked halfheartedly, hoping that she would choose instead to rest after the long bus ride.

"Why not?" Sasha said, and put on her coat.

Boshen folded the sandwich wrapper like a freshly ironed napkin. "I wonder if we could talk for a few minutes here," he said.

Sasha sighed. She never liked Boshen, whom she had met only once and who had struck her as the type of man as fussy as an old hen. She had not hesitated, however, to call him and ask for help when she had found out his number through an acquaintance. She had spoken in a dry, matter-of-fact way about her pregnancy, which had gone too long for an abortion in the state of Nebraska. Yang had fathered the baby; she had told Boshen this first in their phone call. She had had no intention of sparing Boshen the truth; in a way, she felt Boshen was responsible for her misfortune, too.

"Have you, uh, made up your mind about the operation?" Boshen asked.

"What do you think I'm here for?" Sasha said. Over the past week Boshen had called her twice, bringing up the possibility of keeping the baby. Both times she had hung up right away. Whatever interest he had in the baby was stupid and selfish, Sasha had decided.

The easiest solution may not be the best one in life, Boshen thought of telling Sasha, but then, what right did he have to talk about options, when the decisions he had made for his life were all compromises? At thirty-eight, Boshen felt he had achieved less than he had failed. He was a mediocre doctor before he was asked politely to leave the hospital for establishing the first counseling hotline for homosexuals in the small Chinese city where he lived. He moved to Beijing and took on a part-time job at a private clinic while working as an activist for gay rights. After a few visits from the secret police, however, he realized that, in the post-Tiananmen era, talk of any kind of human rights was dangerous. He decided to go into a less extreme and more practical area, advocating for AIDS awareness, but even that he had to give up after pressure from the secret police and his family. He was in love with a boy twenty years younger, and he thought he could make a difference in the boy's life. In the end, he was the one to marry a woman and leave. Boshen had thought of adopting the baby—half of her blood came from Yang, after all—but Sasha's eyes, sharp and unrelenting, chilled him. He smiled weakly and said, "I just wanted to make sure."

Sasha wrapped her head in a shawl and stood up. Boshen did not move, and when she asked him if he was leaving, he said, "I've heard from my friends that Yang is prostituting again." *is that how Sasha got pregnant?*

Not a surprise, Sasha thought, but the man at the table,

too old for a role as a heartbroken lover and too serious for it, was pitiful. In a kinder voice she said, "Then we'll have to live with that, no?"

BOSHEN WAS NOT the first man to have fallen in love with Yang, but he believed, for a long time, that he was the only one to have seen and touched the boy's soul. Since the age of seven, Yang had been trained as a *Nan Dan*—a male actor who plays female roles on stage in the Peking Opera—and had lived his life in the opera school. At seventeen, when he was discovered going out with a male lover, he was expelled. Boshen had written several articles about the incident, but he had not met Yang until he had become a *money boy*. Yang could've easily enticed a willing man to keep him for a good price, but rumors were that the boy was interested only in selling after his first lover abandoned him.

The day Boshen heard about Yang's falling into prostitution, he went to the park where men paid for such services. It was near dusk when he arrived, and men of all ages slipped into the park like silent fish. Soon night fell; beneath the lampposts, transactions started in whispers, familiar scenarios for Boshen, but standing in the shade of a tree—a customer instead of researcher—made him tremble. It was not difficult to recognize Yang in the moon-white-colored silk shirt and pants he was reputed to wear every day to the park. Boshen looked at the boy, too beautiful for the grimy underground, a white lotus blossom untouched by the surrounding mud.

After watching the boy for several days, Boshen finally offered to pay Yang's asking price. The night Yang came home with Boshen, he became drunk on his own words. For a long time he talked about his work, his dream of bringing an end to injustice and building a more tolerant world; Yang huddled on the couch and listened. Boshen thought of shutting up, but the more he talked, the more he despaired at the beautiful and impassive face of Yang—in the boy's eyes he must be the same as all the other men, so full of themselves. Finally Boshen said, "Someday I'll make you go back to the stage."

"An empty promise of a man keeps a woman's heart full," Yang recited in a low voice.

"But this," Boshen said, pointing to the pile of paperwork on his desk. "This is the work that will make it illegal for them to take you away from the stage because of who you are."

Yang's face softened. Boshen watched the unmistakable hope in the boy's eyes. Yang was too young to hide his pain, despite years of wearing female masks and portraying others' tragedies onstage. Boshen wanted to save him from his suffering. After a few weeks of pursuing, Boshen convinced Yang to try a new life. Boshen redecorated the apartment with expensive hand-painted curtains that featured the costumes of the Peking Opera and huge paper lanterns bearing the Peking Opera masks. He sold a few pieces of furniture to make space, and borrowed a rug from a friend for Yang to practice on. Yang fit into the quiet life like the most virtuous woman he had played on stage. He got up early every morning, stretching his body into unbelievable positions, and dancing the most intricate choreography. He trained his voice, too, in the shower so that the neighbors would not hear him. Always Boshen stood outside and listened, Yang's voice splitting the waterfall, the bath curtain, the door, and the rest of the dull world like a silver knife. At those moments Boshen was overwhelmed by gratitude—he was not the only one to have been touched by the boy's beauty, but he was the one to guard and nurture it. That alone lifted him above his mundane, disappointing life.

When Boshen was at work, Yang practiced painting and calligraphy. Sometimes they went out to parties, but most evenings they stayed home. Yang never performed for Boshen, and he dared not ask him to. Yang was an angel falling out of the heavens, and every day Boshen dreaded that he would not be able to return the boy to where he belonged.

Such a fear, as it turned out, was not unfounded. Two months into the relationship, Yang started to show signs of restlessness. During the day he went out more than before, and he totally abandoned painting and calligraphy. Boshen wondered if the boy was suffocated by the stillness of their life.

One day shortly before Boshen was expelled from Beijing and put under house arrest in his hometown, Yang asked him casually how his work was going. Fine, Boshen said, feeling uneasy. Yang had never asked him anything about his work; it was part of the ugly world that Boshen had wanted to shelter Yang from.

"What are you working on?" Yang asked.

"Why, the usual stuff," Boshen said.

"I heard you were working on AIDS," Yang said. "What has that to do with you?"

Stunned, Boshen tried to find an explanation. Finally he said, "You don't understand, Yang."

"I'm not a child," Yang said. "Why are you concerned with that dirty disease? The more you work on it, the more people will connect it with gay people. What good does it do for me?"

"I'm trying to help more people," Boshen said.

"But you've promised to help me get back to the stage," Yang said. "If you insist on working on something irrelevant, you'll never fulfill your promise."

Boshen could not answer Yang. Afterward, Yang started to go out more often, and a few days later, he did not come home for the first time in their relationship. Boshen thought of all the predators waiting to set their fangs and claws on Yang, and he did not sleep that night.

"There's nothing for you to worry about," Yang said with a strange smile when Boshen confronted him. "You're not as endangered as you imagine."

"At least you should've let me know where you were," Boshen said.

"I was with a girl," Yang said, and mentioned the name Sasha, which sounded slightly familiar to Boshen. They had met her at a party, Yang reminded Boshen, but he did not remember who she was; he did not understand why Yang was going out with her, either.

"Why? What a silly question," Yang said. "You do things when you feel like it, no?"

THE FIRST TIME Sasha met Yang, at a party, she felt that she was looking into a mirror that reflected not her own face, but that of someone she could never become. She watched the ballet of his long fingers across the table while he listened absentmindedly to the conversation of others around the table. She looked at the innocent half-moons on his fingernails; her own fingers were plump and blunt. His cream-colored face, his delicate nose and mouth reminded her of an exquisite china doll. Later, when they sat closer, she saw the melancholy in his eyes and decided that he was more like a statue of Kuanyin, the male Buddha in a female body, the goddess who listened and responded to the prayers of suffering women and children. Sitting next to him, Sasha felt like a mass-produced rubber doll.

The uneasy feeling lasted only for a moment. Sasha had heard of his stories, and was glad to see him finally in person. She leaned toward him and asked, as if picking up from a conversation they had dropped somewhere, "What do you think of girls, then?"

He looked up at her, and she saw a strange light in his eyes. They reminded her of a wounded sparrow she had once kept during a cold Mongolian winter. Sparrows were an obstinate species that would never eat and drink once they were caged, her mother told her. Sasha did not believe it. She locked up the bird for days, and it kept bumping into the cage until its head started to go bald. Still she refused to release it, mesmerized by its eyes, wild but helplessly tender, too. She nudged the little bowl of soaked millet closer to the sparrow, but the bird was blind to her hospitality. Cheap birds, a neighbor told her; only cheap birds would be so stubborn. Have a canary, the neighbor said, and she would be singing for you every morning by now.

The boy lowered his eyes at Sasha's scrutiny, and she felt the urge to chase the beautiful eyes, a huntress of that strange light. "You must have known some girls, no?" she said. "When you went to the opera school, were there girls in the school?"

"Yes," the boy said, his voice reminding her of a satin dress.

"So?"

"We didn't talk. They played handmaids and nannies, background roles."

"So you were the princess, huh?" Sasha laughed and saw the boy blush, with anger perhaps, but it made her more curious and insistent in cornering him. "What's your name?" she said.

"Which name?"

"How many names do you have?"

"Two. One given by my parents. One given by the opera school."

"What are they?"

He dipped one finger into a glass of orange juice and wrote on the dark marble tabletop. She followed the wet trace of his finger. It was Yang, a common boy's name with the character for the sun, the masculine principle of nature, the opposite of Yin.

"A so-so name. What's your opera name?"

"Sumeng," he said. A serene and pure dreamer, it meant.

"Worse. Sounds like a weepy name from a romance novel," Sasha said. "You need a better name. I'll have to think of one for you."

In the end she did not use either name, and did not find a better one for him. She called him "my little *Nan Dan*," and that was what he was to her, a boy destined to play a woman's part. She paged him often, and invited him to movies and walks in the park. She made decisions for them both, and he let her. She tried to pry him open with questions—she was so curious about him—and slowly he started to talk, about the man he had loved and men who loved him. He never said anything about the opera school or his stage life, and she

(77)

learned not to push him. He was so vain, Sasha thought
when he spent a long time fixing his hair or when he put on
an expression of aloofness at the slightest attention of a
stranger; she teased him, and then felt tender and guilty
when he did not defend himself. She made fun of the other
people in Yang's life, too: his lover, Boshen, whom she believed to be a useless dreamer, and the men who boldly asked
him for his number. She believed she was the first person in
his life who did not worship him in any way, and he must be
following her around because of that. It pleased her.

Was she dating the boy? Sasha's classmates asked when
they saw her with Yang more than once. Of course not, she
said. In a month, Sasha was to go to America for graduate
school, and it was pointless to start a relationship now. Besides, how smart was it to date a boy who loved no one but
himself?

EVEN THE WIND could not cut through the warm bodies
lined up on both sides of Michigan Avenue. Sasha pushed
through the crowd. They looked so young and carefree,
these Americans, happy as a group of pupils on a field trip.
She envied these people, who would stand in a long line in
front of a popcorn shop waiting for a bag of fresh popcorn,
lovers leaning into each other, children hanging on to their
parents. They were born to be themselves, naive and contented with their naivety.

"I would trade my place with any one of them," Sasha
said to Boshen, but when he raised his voice and asked her
to repeat her words, she shook her head. If only there were
a law in America binding her to where her baby belonged so
that the baby would have a reason to live!

Sasha herself had once been used by the law to trap her

mother in the grassland. One of the thousands of high school students sent down from Beijing to Inner Mongolia for labor reeducation, her mother, in order to join the Party, married a Mongolian herdsman, one of the model interracial marriages that were broadcast across the grassland. Five years later, at the end of the Cultural Revolution, all of the students were allowed to return to Beijing. Sasha's mother, however, was forced to stay, even after she divorced her Mongolian husband. Their two daughters, born in the grassland, did not have legal residency in Beijing, and the mother had to stay where the children belonged. *) wow*

Sasha pushed forward, looking at every store window. Silky scarves curved around the mannequins' necks with soft obedience. Diamonds glistened on dark velvet. At a street corner, children gathered and watched the animated story displayed in the windows of Marshall Field's. If only her baby were a visa that would admit her into this prosperity, Sasha thought, saddened by the memories of Nebraska and Inner Mongolia, the night skies of both places black with lonely, lifeless stars.

"There's an open spot there," Boshen said. "Do you want to stand there?"

Sasha nodded, and Boshen followed her. Apart from the brief encounter at the party in Beijing and a few phone calls, he did not know her. He had thought about her often after she had called him about the pregnancy. What kind of girl, he had wondered, would've made Yang a father? He had imagined a mature and understanding girl. Beautiful, too. He had made up a perfect woman for Yang and for his own peace of mind, but Sasha had disappointed him. When they settled along the curb, he said, "So, what's your plan after the operation?"

Sasha stood on tiptoe like a child, and looked in the direction where the parade would start. Boshen regretted right away speaking with such animosity. Seeing nothing, she turned to him and said, "What's *your* plan in America? Where's your new wife, anyway?"

Boshen frowned. He had told Yang that the marriage would be used as a cover, and his departure was meant only to be a temporary one. He had promised Yang other things, too, money he would send, help he would seek in the overseas Chinese community for Yang's return to the stage. Not a day since he had arrived did he forget his promises, but Sasha's words stung him. His marriage must have been an unforgivable betrayal, in Sasha's and Yang's eyes alike. "I can't defend myself," Boshen said finally.

"Of course not. You were the one sending him back to the street," Sasha said.

"It's been a troubled time," Boshen said, struggling over the words. "It's been difficult for all of us. But we certainly should try to help him out."

Sasha turned to look at Boshen with an amused smile. "You speak like the worst kind of politician," she said. "Show me the solution."

"I am thinking." Boshen hesitated, and said, "I've been thinking—if we can tell him that he'll be able to perform in America, maybe he would want to leave Beijing?"

"And then?"

"We will try here. There's a *Nan Dan* master in New York. Maybe we can contact him and ask for his help. But the first thing we do is to get Yang out of the country."

"Does that 'we' include me?"

"If you could marry Yang, he would be here in no time. I

know him. If there's one percent chance to go back to the stage, he'll try."

"A very nice plan, Boshen," Sasha said. "But why should I agree to the proposal? What's in it for me?"

Boshen looked away from Sasha and watched a couple kiss at the other side of the street. After a long moment, he turned to Sasha and tried to look into her eyes. "You must have loved him at least once, Sasha," he said, his voice trembling.

SASHA HAD NOT planned for love, or even an affair. The friendship was out of whimsy, a convenience for the empty days immediately before graduating from college. The movie they watched one night in July was not planned, either. It was ten o'clock when Sasha purchased the tickets, at the last minute. Yang looked at the clock in the ticket booth and wondered aloud if it was too late, and Sasha laughed, asking him if he was a child and if his lover had a curfew for him.

The movie was *Pretty Woman*, with almost unreadable Chinese subtitles. When they came out to the midnight street, Sasha said, "Don't you just love Julia Roberts?"

"What's to love about her?" Yang said.

Sasha glanced at Yang. He was quiet throughout the movie—he did not understand English, but Sasha thought at least he could've enjoyed the beautiful actress. "She's pretty, and funny, and so—American," Sasha said. "America is a good place. Everything could happen there. A prostitute becomes a princess; a crow turns into a swan overnight."

"A prostitute never becomes a princess," Yang said.

"How do you know?" Sasha said. "If only you could come with me to America and take a look at it yourself."

After a long moment, Yang said, "Every place is a good place. Only time goes wrong."

Sasha said nothing. She did not want to spend the night philosophizing. When they walked past a small hotel, she asked Yang if he wanted to come in with her. Just for the fun of staying out for a night, she said; he needn't have to report to his lover anyway, she added. Yang hesitated, and she grabbed his hand and pulled him into the foyer with her. A middle-aged woman at the reception opened the window and said, "What do you want?"

"Comrade, do you have a single room for two persons?" Sasha said.

The woman threw out a pad for registration and shut the window. Sasha filled in the form. The woman scanned the pad. "Your ID?" she asked.

Sasha handed her ID to the woman. The woman looked at it for a long time, and pointed to Yang with her chin. "His ID?"

"He's my cousin from Inner Mongolia," Sasha said in a cheerful voice. "He forgot to bring his ID with him."

"Then there's no room tonight." The woman threw out Sasha's ID and closed the window.

"Comrade." Sasha tapped on the glass.

The woman opened the window. "Go away," she said. "Your cousin? Let me tell you—either you have a marriage license and I will give you a room, or you go out and do that shameless thing in the street and let the cops arrest you. Don't you think I don't know girls like you?"

Sasha dragged Yang out the door, his lips quavering. "I don't believe I can't find a room for us," Sasha said finally.

Yang looked at Sasha with a baffled look. "Why do we have to do this?" he said.

"Ha, you're afraid now. Go ahead if you don't want to come," Sasha said, and started to walk. Yang followed Sasha to an even smaller hotel at the end of a narrow lane. An old man was sitting behind a desk, playing poker with himself. "Grandpapa," Sasha said, handing her ID to the old man. "Do you have a single room for my brother and me?"

The old man looked at Sasha and then Yang. "He's not fifteen yet so he doesn't have an ID," Sasha said, and Yang smiled shyly at the old man, his white teeth flashing in the dark.

The old man nodded and handed a registration pad to Sasha. Five minutes later they were granted a key. It was a small room on the second floor, with two single beds, a rusty basin stand with two basins, and a window that did not have a curtain. Roaches scurried to find a hiding place when Sasha turned on the light. They stood just inside the door, and all of a sudden she did not know what the excitement was of spending a night together in a filthy hotel. "Why don't we just go home?" Yang said behind her.

"Where's the place you call home?" Sasha snapped. She turned off the light and lay down on a bed without undressing. "Go back to the man who keeps you if this is not a place for a princess like you," she said.

Yang stood for a long moment before he got into the other bed. Sasha waited for him to speak, and when he did not, she became angry with him, and with herself.

The next morning, when the city stirred to life, they both lay awake in their own beds. The homing pigeons flew across the sky, the small brass whistles bound to their tails humming in a harmonious low tone. Not far away, Tao music played on a tape recorder, calling for the early risers to join the practice of tai chi. Old men, the fans of Peking Opera, sang their favorite parts of the opera, their voices cracking at high notes. Then the doors down the lane creaked open, releasing the shouting children headed to school, and adults to work, their bicycle bells clanking.

Later, someone turned on a record player and music blasted across the alley. Sasha sat up and looked out the window. A young man was setting up a newspaper stand at the end of the alley, making theatrical movements along with a song in which a rock singer was yelling, "Oh, Genghis Khan, Genghis Khan, he's a powerful old man. He's rich, he's strong, and I want to marry him."

Sasha listened to the song repeat and said, "I don't understand why these people think they have the right to trash Genghis Khan."

"Their ears are dead to real music," Yang said.

"When I was little, my father taught me a song about Genghis Khan. It's the only Mongolian song I remember now," Sasha said, and opened her mouth to sing the song. The melody was in her mind, but no words came to her tongue. She had forgotten almost all of the Mongolian words she had learned, after her parents' divorce; she had not seen her father for fifteen years. "Well, I don't remember it anymore."

"*The broken pillars, the slanted roof, they once saw the banqueting days; the dying trees, the withering peonies, they once danced in the heavenly music. The young girls dreamed of their lovers who were enlisted to fight the Huns. They did not know the loved ones had become white bones glistening in the moonlight,*" Yang chanted in a low voice to the ceiling. "Our masters say that real arts never die. Real arts are about remembrance."

"What's the point of remembering the song anyway? I don't even remember what my father looked like." Sasha thought about her father, one of the offspring of Genghis Khan. Genghis Khan was turned into a clown in the pop song. Mongolia was once the biggest empire in the world, and now it was a piece of meat, sandwiched by China and Russia.

"We live in a wrong time," Yang said.

Sasha turned to look at Yang. He lay on his hands and stared at the ceiling, his face taking on the resigned look of an old man. It hurt her, and scared her too, to glimpse a world beneath his empty beauty. "We were born into a wrong place, is what our problem is," she said, trying to cheer him and herself up. "Why don't you come to America with me, Yang?"

Yang smiled. "Who am I to follow you?"

"A husband, a lover, a brother, I don't care. Why don't you get out of Beijing and have a new life in America?" The words, once said, hung in the room like heavy fog, and Sasha wondered if Yang, too, had difficulty breathing. Outside the window, a vendor was sharpening a chopper with a whetstone, the strange sound making their mouths water unpleasantly. Then the vendor started to sing in a drawn-out voice about his tasty pig heads.

"Sasha," Yang said finally. "Is Sasha a Mongolian name?"

"Not really. It's Russian, a name of my mom's favorite heroine in a Soviet war novel."

"That's why it doesn't sound Chinese. I would rather it is a Mongolian name," Yang said. "Sasha, the princess of Mongolia."

Sasha walked barefoot to Yang's bed and knelt beside

him. He did not move, and let Sasha hold his face with both hands. "Come to America with me," she said. "We'll be the prince and the princess of Nebraska."

"I was not trained to play a prince," Yang said.

"The script is changed," Sasha said. "From today on."

Yang turned to look at Sasha. She tried to kiss him, but he pushed her away gently. "*A beautiful body is only a bag of bones,*" he sang in a low voice.

Sasha had never seen Yang perform, and could not imagine him onstage; he had played princesses and prostitutes, but he did not have to live with the painted mask and the silk costume. "The Peking Opera is dead," she said. "Why don't you give it up?"

"Who are you to say that about the Peking Opera?" Yang said, his face turning suddenly stern.

Sasha saw the iciness in Yang's eyes and let the topic drop. Afterward, neither mentioned anything about the stay in the hotel. A week later, when Boshen was escorted away from Beijing, Sasha was relieved and scared. There was, all of a sudden, time for them to fill. To her relief and disappointment, Yang seemed to have forgotten the moment when they were close, so close that they were almost in love.

THE PARADE STARTED with music and laughter, colorful floats moving past, on which happy people waved to the happy audience. Boshen looked at Sasha's face, lit up by curiosity, and sighed. Despite her willfulness and unfriendliness, the thought of the baby—Yang's baby—made him eager to forgive her. "Do you still not want to tell Yang about the baby?" he said.

"You've asked this the hundredth time," Sasha said. "Why should I?"

"He might want to come to the U.S. if he learned about the baby," Boshen said.

"There'll be no baby after tomorrow," Sasha said. She had tried Yang's phone number when she had learned of the pregnancy; she had tried his pager, too. At first it was measured by hours and days, and then it became weeks since she had left the message on his pager. He might be living in another apartment with a new telephone number. The pager might no longer belong to him. She knew he had every reason for not getting her message, but she could not forgive his silence. In the meantime, her body changed. She felt the growth inside her and she was disgusted by it. Sometimes she hated it from morning till night, hoping that it would finally go away, somehow, surrendering to the strength of her resentment. Other times she kept her mind away for as long as she could, thinking that it would disappear as if it had never existed. Still, in the end, it required her action. In the end, she thought, it was just a chunk of flesh and blood.

"But why was there a baby in the first place?" Boshen said. Why and how it happened were the questions that had been haunting him since he had heard from Sasha. He wanted to ask her if she, too, had been dazzled by the boy's body, smooth, lithe, perfectly shaped. He wanted to know if she had loved him as he had, but in that case, how could she have the heart to discard what had been left with her?

Sasha turned to Boshen. For the first time, she studied the man with curiosity. Not handsome or ugly, he had a candid face that Sasha thought she could not fall in love with but nonetheless could trust. A man like Boshen should have an ordinary life, boring and comfortable, yet his craze for Yang made him a more interesting man than he deserved to be. But that must be what was Yang's value—he made people fall in love with him, and the love led them astray, willingly, from their otherwise tedious paths. Yang had been the one to bring up the idea of spending a night together again, and Sasha the one to ask a friend for the use of her rented room, a few days before Sasha's flight. It was one of the soggiest summer evenings. After their lovemaking, sweet and short and uneventful, they stayed on the floor, on top of the blanket Sasha had brought for the purpose, an arm's length between them, each too warm to touch the other. Outside, the landlady's family and two other neighbor families were sitting in the courtyard and watching a TV program, their voices mixed with the claps of their hands killing the mosquitoes. Sasha turned to look at Yang, who was lying with his back to her. The little pack of condoms she had bought was tucked underneath the blanket, unopened. She had suggested it and he had refused. A rubber was for people who touched without loving each other, Yang had said; his words had made her hopeful again. "Do you want to come to America with me now?" she asked, tracing his back with one finger.

"What am I going to do in America? Be kept as a canary by you?" Yang said and moved farther away from her finger.

"You can spend some time learning English, and get a useful degree in America."

"Useful? Don't you already know that I am useless? Besides, nothing humiliates a man more than living as a parasite on his woman," Yang said, and reached for a silk robe he had packed with him. Before Sasha had the time to stop him, he walked out the door. Sasha jumped to her feet and watched from behind the curtain; Yang walked with a calculated laziness, not looking at the people who turned their eyes away from the television to stare at him. When he reached the brick sink in the middle of the courtyard, he sat on the edge and raised his bare legs to the tap. The water had run for a long moment before the landlady recovered from her shock and said, "Hey, the water costs me money."

Yang smiled. "It's so hot," he said in a pleasant voice.

"Indeed," the landlady agreed.

Yang turned off the tap and walked back to the room, with the same grace and idleness, knowing that the people in the courtyard were all watching him, his willowy body wrapped in the moon white robe. Sasha stood by the window, cold with disappointment. She became his audience, one of the most difficult to capture, perhaps, but he succeeded after all.

A Disney float approached the corner where Sasha and Boshen stood. "Look," Sasha said and pointed at a giant glove of Mickey Mouse moving ahead of the float. "There're only four fingers."

"I didn't know that," Boshen said.

"Yang needs us no more than that glove needs us for our admiration," Sasha said.

"But our love is the only thing to protect him, and to save him, too."

Sasha turned and looked into Boshen's eyes. "It's people like us who have destroyed him, isn't it? Why was there *Nan Dan* in the Peking Opera in the first place? *Men loved him because he was playing a woman; women loved him because he was a man playing,*" she said.

"That's totally wrong."

"Why else do you want so much to put him back on the stage? Don't think I'm happy to see him fall. Believe me, I wanted to help him as much as you do. He didn't have to be a man playing a woman—I thought I would make him understand. But what did I end up with? You're not the one who has a baby inside; he's not the one having an abortion," Sasha said, and started to cry.

Boshen held out his hand and touched Sasha's shoulder hesitantly. If only she could love the boy one more time. Yang could choose to live with either of them; he could choose not to love them at all but their love would keep him safe and intact; they could—the three of them—bring up the baby together. Yang would remain the princess, exiled, yes, but a true princess, beautiful in a foreign land. If only he knew how to make Sasha love Yang again, Boshen thought.

Sasha did not move away when Boshen put an arm around her shoulder. They must look like the most ordinary couple to strangers, a nervous husband comforting his moody wife after an argument. They might as well be a couple, out of love, he caring only for the baby inside her, she having no feeling left for anything, her unborn child included.

As if responding, the baby moved. A tap, and then another one, gentle and tentative, the first greeting that Sasha had wished she would never have to answer, but it seemed impossible, once it happened, not to hope for more. After a long moment, people in the street shouted, and children screamed out of excitement. Sasha looked up—the lights were lit up in the trees, thousands of stars forming a constellation. She thought about the small Mongolian town where her mother lived alone now, her long shadow trailing behind her as she walked home along the dimly lit alley. Her mother had been born into a wrong time, lived all her adult life in a wrong place, yet she had never regretted the births of her two daughters. Sasha held her breath and waited for more of the baby's messages. America was a good country, she thought, a right place to be born into, even though the baby had come at a wrong time. Everything was possible in America, she thought, and imagined a baby possessing the beauty of her father but happier, and luckier. Sasha smiled, but then when the baby moved again, she burst into tears. Being a mother must be the saddest yet the most hopeful thing in the world, falling into a love that, once started, would never end.

Is she gonna keep it?

she wants a love that will never end.

Love in the Marketplace

SANSAN IS KNOWN TO HER STUDENTS AS MISS Casablanca. A beautiful nickname if one does not pay attention to the cruel, almost malicious smiles when the name is mentioned, and she chooses not to see. Sansan, at thirty-two, does not have a husband, a lover, or a close friend. Since graduation from college, she has been teaching English at the Educators' School in the small town where she grew up, a temporary job that has turned permanent. For ten years she has played *Casablanca*, five or six times a semester, for each class of students. The pattern of their response has become familiar, and thus bearable for her. At the beginning, they watch in awe, it being the first real American movie they have watched, without Chinese dubbing or subtitles. Sansan sees them struggle to understand the dialogue, but the most they can do is catch a phrase or two now and then. Still, they seem to have no trouble understanding the movie, and always, some girls end the class with red teary eyes. But soon they lose their interest. They laugh when the women in the movie cry; they whistle when a man kisses a woman on the screen. In the end, Sansan watches the movie alone, with the added sound track from the chatting students.

That is what Sansan is doing with her morning class when someone taps on the door. Only when the knocking becomes urgent does she pause the tape.

"Your mother's waiting for you outside. She wants to see you," the janitor says when Sansan opens the door.

"What for?"

"She didn't say."

"Can't you see I'm busy with my students?"

"It's your mother waiting outside," the janitor says, one foot planted firmly inside the door.

Sansan stares at the janitor. After a moment, she sighs. "OK, tell her I'm coming," she says. The students all watch on amused. She tells them to keep watching the movie, and knows they will not.

Outside the school gate, Sansan finds her mother leaning onto the wooden wheelbarrow she pushes to the marketplace every day. Stacked in it are a coal stove, a big aluminum pot, packs of eggs, bottles of spices, and a small wooden stool. For forty years, Sansan's mother has been selling hard-boiled eggs in the marketplace by the train station, mostly to travelers. Sitting on the stool for all her adult life has made her a tiny stooped woman. Sansan hasn't seen her mother for a year, since her father's funeral. Her mother's hair is thinner and grayer, but so will Sansan's own be in a few years, and she feels no sentiment for either of them.

"Mama, I heard you were looking for me," Sansan says.

"How else would I know that you're alive?"

"Why? I thought people talked about me to you all the time."

"They can lie to me."

"Of course." Sansan grins.

"But whose problem is it when you make people talk about you?"

"Theirs."

"You've never known how to spell the word 'shame.' "

"Do you come just to tell me that I should be ashamed of myself? I know it by heart now."

"What god did I offend to deserve you as a daughter?" Her mother raises her voice. A few passersby slow down and look at them with amused smiles.

"Mama, do you have something to say? I'm busy."

"It won't be long before you will become an orphan, Sansan. One day I'll be drowned by all the talk about you."

"People's words don't kill a person."

"What killed your dad, then?"

"I was not the only disappointment for dad," Sansan says. Hard as she tries, she feels her throat squeezed tight by a sudden grief. Her father, before his death, worked as a meter reader, always knocking on people's doors around din- nertime, checking their gas and water meters, feeling re- sponsible for the ever-rising rates and people's anger. One evening he disappeared after work. Later he was discovered by some kids in a pond outside the town, his body planted upside down. The pond was shallow, waist deep at most; he had plunged himself into the mud, with the force of a leap maybe, but nobody could tell for sure how he did it, or why. Sansan's mother believed that it was Sansan's failure at mar- riage that killed him.

"Think of when you first went to college. Your dad and I thought we were the most accomplished parents in the world," her mother says, ready to reminisce and cry.

"Mama, we've been there many times. Let's not talk about it."

"Why? You think I toil all these years just to raise a daughter to shut me up?"

"I'm sorry, but I have to go," Sansan says.

"Don't go yet. Stay with me longer," her mother says, almost pleading.

Sansan tries to soften her voice. "Mama, I'm in the middle of a class."

"Come home tonight, then. I have something important to tell you."

"Why don't you tell me now? I can spare five minutes."

"Five minutes are not enough. It's about Tu." Sansan's mother steps closer and whispers, "Tu is divorced."

Sansan stares at her mother for a long moment. Her mother nods at her. "Yes, he's unoccupied now."

"I don't know what you're talking about," Sansan says.

"His parents want you to go back to him."

"Mama, I don't understand."

"That's why you have to come home and talk to me. Now go teach," Sansan's mother says, and pushes the wheelbarrow forward before Sansan replies.

SANSAN DISCOVERED *CASABLANCA* the year Tu wrote a short and apologetic letter from America, explaining his decision not to marry her. Before the letter's arrival, she showed *The Sound of Music* to her students, humming with every song, ready to abandon the students for America at any minute. After the letter, she has never sung again. *Casablanca* says all she wants to teach the students about life.

Sansan goes back to the classroom and resumes her

place on the windowsill, letting her legs dangle the way she remembers her American teachers did in college. At the end of the Paris scene, when Rick gets soaked on the platform in the pouring rain, and then boards the train, a boy says, "How funny. His coat is dry as a camel's fur now."

Sansan is surprised that she has missed the detail all along. She thinks of praising the boy for his keen observation, but changes her mind. "One of life's mysteries is its inexplicability," she raises her voice and says.

The students roar with laughter. Certainly the line will be passed on, along with the nickname, to the next class, but Sansan does not care. The students, recent graduates from junior high, will be teaching elementary students after the two years of studying in the Educators' School. Most of them are from villages, and the school is their single chance to escape heavy farm labor. English is taught only to comply with a regulation set by the Education Department; they will never understand what she means, these kids living out their petty desires.

After two classes, Sansan decides to take off, complaining to her colleagues of a headache. Nobody believes her excuse, she knows, but nobody would contradict her, either. They indulge her the way people do a person with a mild and harmless craziness, whose eccentricity adds color to their otherwise dull lives. Among the few people in town who have college degrees, Sansan is the best-educated one. She was one of the two children from the town who have ever made it to the most prestigious college in Beijing, and the only one to have returned. The other one, Tu, the childhood companion and classmate and boyfriend and fiancé at one time or another in her life, is in America, married to a woman more beautiful than Sansan.

And divorced now, ten years too late. Back in her rented room, Sansan sits on her bed and cracks sunflower seeds. The shells rain down onto the sheet and the floor, and she lets them pile up. She craves the popping sounds in her skull, and the special flavor in her mouth. It is the sunflower seeds, sweet and salty and slightly bitter from the nameless spices Gong's Dried Goods Shop uses to process its sunflower seeds, and the English novels she bought in college— a full shelf of them, each one worthy of someone's lifetime to study—that make her life bearable. But the sunflower seeds taste different today; Tu's divorce, like a fish bone stabbed in her throat, distracts her.

Tu would never imagine her sitting among the shells of sunflower seeds and pondering his failed marriage, but she still imagines him on a daily basis. Not a surprise, as she promised Tu at their engagement ceremony. "I'll be thinking of you until the day when all the seas in the world dry up," she said. Tu must have said something similar, and Min, the only witness of the ceremony and then Tu's legal wife on paper, hugged both of them. It was odd, in retrospect, that Min did not take a vow. After all, the engagement between Sansan and Tu, just as the marriage between Min and Tu, was the contract for all three of them.

Min was the most beautiful girl Sansan had met in college, and is, ten years later, the most beautiful person in her memory. In college they lived in the same dorm with four other girls, but for a long time in their first year, they were not close. Min was a city girl, attractive, outgoing, one of the girls who would have anything they set their eyes on, and of course they only set their eyes on the best. Sansan, a girl from a small town, with a heavy accent and a plain face, was far from the best for Min, as a confidante or a friend.

Toward the end of their freshman year, the demonstrations in Tiananmen Square disrupted their study. Min became an active protester in the Square. Miss Tiananmen, the boys voted her; she dressed up as the Statue of Liberty and gestured victory to the Western reporters' cameras. After the crashing down, she had to go through a difficult time, being checked and rechecked; she ended up belonging to the category that did not need imprisonment but did not have a right to any legal job after graduation, either. When Min came back to school, still beautiful but sad and defeated, Sansan was the first and the only person in the dorm who dared to express sympathy and friendliness toward Min. Sansan was among the few who had not attended any protests. She and Tu had been the only students showing up for classes when their classmates had gone on a strike; later, when the teachers had stopped coming to classes, they had become intimate, falling in love as their parents and the whole town back home had expected them to.

Sansan never thought of her friendly gesture to Min as anything noble or brave; it was out of a simple wish to be nice to someone who deserved a better treatment from life. Sansan was overwhelmed with joy and gratitude, then, when Min decided to return the goodwill and become her best friend. Sansan felt a little uneasy, too, as if she had taken advantage of Min's bad fortune; they would have never become friends under normal circumstances, but then, what was wrong with living with the exceptional, if that's what was given by life?

At the end of their sophomore year, the Higher Education Department announced a new policy that allowed only those students who had American relatives to be granted passports for studying abroad, something that made no sense at all, but such was their life at the time, living with all the ridiculous rules that changed their lives like a willy-nilly child. Min's only hope for her future—going to America after graduation—became a burst bubble, and Sansan, when she could not stand the heartbreakingly beautiful face of Min, started to think and act with resolution.

"Are you out of your mind?" Tu said when she announced to him her plan—that he would apply to an American graduate school and help Min out through a false marriage. "I don't have any American relatives."

"Your grandfather's brother—didn't he go to Taiwan after the Liberation War? Why couldn't he have gone to America later? Listen, nobody will go to America to check your family history. As long as we get a certificate saying that he's in America . . ."

"But who'll give us the certificate?"

"I'll worry about that. You think about the application," Sansan said. She saw the hesitation in Tu's eyes, but there was also a spark of hope, and she caught it before it dimmed. "Don't you want to go to America, too? We don't have to go back home after graduation, and work at some boring jobs because we don't have city residency. Nobody will care about whether you are from a small town when you get to America."

"But to marry Min?"

"Why not?" Sansan said. "We have each other, but she doesn't have anyone. The city boys—they all become turtles in their shells once she's in trouble."

Tu agreed to try. It was one of the reasons Sansan loved him—he trusted her despite his own doubt; he followed her decision. Persuading Min seemed easy, even though she too questioned the plan. Sansan alone nudged Tu and Min toward the collective American dream for all three of them; she went back to her hometown, and through bribing and pleading got a false certificate about the American grand-uncle of Tu. The plan could have gone wrong but it went right at every step. Tu was accepted by a school in Pennsylvania; Min, with the marriage certificate, got her own paperwork done to leave the country as Tu's dependent. The arrange-ment, a secret known only to the three of them, was too com-plicated to explain to outsiders, but none of the three had a doubt then. One more year and the plan would be complete, when Min would find a way to sponsor herself, and Tu, with a marriage and a divorce under his belt, would come home and marry Sansan.

It did not occur to Sansan that she should have had sex with Tu before he took off. In fact, he asked for it, but she refused. She remembered reading, in her college course, *Women in Love,* and one detail had stuck with her ever since. One of the sisters, before her lover went to war, re-fused to have sex with him, afraid that it would make him crave women at a time when only death was available. But Tu was not going to a war but a married life with another woman. How could a man resist falling in love with a beau-tiful woman whose body ate, slept, peed, and menstruated in the same apartment, a thin door away from him?

Sansan started to imagine the lovemaking between Tu and Min when, after the short letter informing her of their intention to stay in the marriage, neither would write to her again. She stripped them, put them in bed, and studied their sex as if it would give her an answer. Min's silky long hair brushed against the celery stalk of Tu's body, teasing him, calling out to him; Tu pushed his large cauliflower head against Min's heavy breasts, a hungry, ugly piglet looking for his nourishment. The more she imagined, the more absurd they became. It was unfair of her, Sansan knew, to make Tu into a comic image, but Min's beauty, like a diamond, was impenetrable. Sansan had never worried about the slightest possibility of their falling in love—Min was too glamorous a girl for Tu, the boy with a big head, a thin body, and a humble smile. She had put her faith in the love between Tu and herself, and she had believed in the sacrifice they had to go through to save a friend. But inexplicable as life was, Min and Tu fell in love, and had mismatched sex in Sansan's mind. Sometimes she replaced Min with herself, and masturbated. Tu and she looked more harmonious—they had been playmates when Sansan had been a toddler sitting by her mother's stove, where Tu had been a small boy from the next stall, the fruit vendor's son; the sex, heartbreakingly beautiful, made her cry afterward.

Sansan took up the habit of eating sunflower seeds when she could no longer stand her imagination. Every night, she sits for hours cracking sunflower seeds; she reaches for the bag the first thing when she wakes up, before she gets out of bed. She calms down when the shells pop in her brain, and is able to imagine Tu and Min in their clothes. The fact that they both broke their promises to her, hurtful as it is and it will always be, no longer matters. What remains meaningful is Tu and Min's marriage vows to each other. She was the one to make them husband and wife, and even if they would be too ashamed to admit it to each other, she would always hover above their marriage bed, a guardian angel that blesses and curses them with her forgiveness.

What, then, has led them to end their marriage, ten years

too late? Once they broke their promises to her; twice they did. With a divorce, what will become of her, when neither of them will be obliged to think about her nobleness?

WHEN THE BAG of sunflower seeds runs out, Sansan decides to go find her mother and ask about Tu's divorce. The marketplace, the only one in town, is next to the railway station. The trains running between Beijing and the southern cities stop several times a day at the station for ten-minute breaks, and many vendors rely on these trains for their businesses.

The one-fifteen train has just pulled into the station when Sansan arrives. A few passengers show up stretching their legs and arms, and soon more flood into the marketplace. Sansan stands a few steps away and watches her mother hitting the side of the pot with a steel ladle and chanting, "Come and try—come and buy—the eight-treasure eggs—the best you'll ever taste."

A woman stops and lifts the lid, and her kid points to the biggest egg in the pot. More people slow down at the good smell of tea leaves, spices, and soy sauce. Some take out their wallets to pay; others, seeing more egg sellers, walk on without knowing they've missed the best hard-boiled eggs in the world. When Sansan was young, she was infuriated by the people who did not choose her mother's eggs—the other vendors were all stingy, never adding as many spices and tea leaves to their pots as her mother did. But when Sansan became older, she grew angry, instead, at her mother's stubbornness. All those people who buy her eggs—strangers that come and go and will not remember this place or her mother's face even if they remember the taste of the eggs—

they will never know that her mother spends more money on the best spices and tea leaves.

When the train leaves, Sansan finds a brick and puts it next to her mother's stool. She sits down and watches her mother add eggs and more spices to the pot. "Isn't it a waste of money to put in so much of the expensive spices?" Sansan says.

"Don't tell me how to boil eggs. I have done this for forty years, and have brought you up boiling eggs my way."

"But even if people can taste the difference, they will never come back to look for your eggs."

"Why not give them their one chance to eat the best eggs in the world, then?" her mother says, raising her voice. A few vendors look at them, winking at one another. The marketplace is full of eyes and ears. By dinnertime, the whole town will have known that Sansan has shown up and attacked her poor mother, and children of the town will be warned, at the dinner tables, not to follow Sansan's example, a daughter not fulfilling her filial duty, who spends money on renting when her mother has kept a room ready for her.

"Mama, why don't you think of retirement?" Sansan says in a lower voice.

"Who will feed me then, a poor old widow?"

"I will."

"You don't even know how to take care of yourself," her mother says. "What you need is a man like Tu."

Sansan looks at her own shadow on the ground, and the fragments of eggshells by her leather sandals. The eggshells were her only toys before she befriended Tu from the next stall, the fruit vendor's son. Tu's parents have retired, living in a two-bedroom flat that Tu bought for them. The next stall now sells cigarettes and lighters and palm-sized pictures of blond women whose clothes, when put close to the flame, disappear. After a moment, Sansan asks, "What happened to Tu?"

"His parents came by yesterday, and asked if you wanted to go back to him."

"Why?"

"A man needs a woman. You need a husband, too."

"Is that what I am, a substitute?"

"Don't act willful. You're not a young girl anymore."

"Why did he get a divorce?"

"People change their minds. Sansan, if you ask me, I would say just go back to Tu without questioning."

"Is that what Tu wants? Or is it his parents' idea?"

"What's the difference? He'll marry you if you want to go back to him, that's what his parents said."

"That would make it an arranged marriage."

"Nonsense. We've seen you two grow up together from the beginning," Sansan's mother says. "Even in arranged marriages, people fall in love."

Sansan feels a sting in her heart. "Sure, people fall in love in arranged marriages, but that's not the love I want."

"What do you want, then, Miss Romantic?"

Sansan does not reply. A romance is more than a love story with a man. A promise is a promise, a vow remains a vow; such is the grandeur of *Casablanca,* such is the true romance that keeps every day of her life meaningful.

Neither of them speaks. Sansan watches her mother pick up the fresh eggs with the ladle, and crack the shells carefully with a spoon so that the spices will soak the eggs well. When her mother finishes, she scoops up an egg and puts it into Sansan's hands without a word. The egg is hot but

Sansan does not drop it. She looks at the cracks on the shell, darkened by the spices and soy sauce like a prophet's fractured turtle shell. When she was younger, she had to beg her mother for a long time before she was given an egg to eat, but when Tu was around, her mother always gave them each an egg without hesitation. Sansan wonders if her mother still remembers such things, the nourishing of their relationship long before she and Tu became lovers.

A FEW MINUTES pass, and then, across the street, two jeeps stop with screeching noises. Sansan looks up and sees several cops jump out and surround Gong's Dried Goods Shop. Soon the customers are driven out the door. "What's going on?" the vendors ask one another. Sansan's mother stands up and looks across the street for a minute, and hands the ladle to Sansan. "Take care of the stove for me," her mother says, and walks across the street with a few other curious vendors.

Sansan watches her mother pushing to the front of the store, where the cops have set up red warning tapes. She wonders why, after forty years in the marketplace, her mother is still interested in other people's business.

Ten minutes later, her mother returns and says to the vendors, "You'll never imagine this—they've found opium in Gong's goods."

"What?"

"No wonder their business is always so good—they add opium when they make their nuts and seeds so people will always want to go back to them," Sansan's mother says. "What black-hearted people they are!"

"How did the police find out?" the vendor across the aisle asks.

"Someone working in the shop must have told on them."

More vendors come back. Sansan listens to them talking about Gong's opium business, her palms wet and sticky. She was planning to go to Gong's to buy more sunflower seeds before the end of the day; even the thought of the sunflower seeds makes her eager to go home and hide herself in a pile of cracked shells, letting the taste on her tongue take her over and carry her away to a safe place, where she watches over Tu and Min serenely. Is that what she is living on, a poisoned food, a drugged dream?

Sansan's mother turns to her. "But let's not talk about other people's trouble. What do you think of the proposal, Sansan?"

"To marry Tu? No, I don't want to marry him."

"You've been waiting for him all these years. Don't be silly."

"I've never waited for him."

"But that's a lie. Everyone knows you're waiting for him."

"Everyone?"

"Why else do you never get married? Everyone knows he did this horrible thing to you, but men make mistakes. Even his parents apologized yesterday. It's time to think about forgiveness.") what about his apology loi.

"What's to forgive?"

"He *had* you, and then left you for another woman. Listen, it would not be that bad a thing if you went back to him. As the old saying goes—*what belongs to someone will belong to him eventually.*"

"Wait a minute, Mama. What do you mean he had me?"

Sansan's mother blushes. "You know what I mean."

"No, I don't know. If you mean sex, no, he's never had me."

"There's nothing to be ashamed of. It was understandable, and it was nobody's fault."

Sansan, for the first time, understands the town's tolerance of her, a pitiful woman used and then abandoned by a lover, a woman unmarriable because she will never be able to demonstrate her virginity on the snow-white sheet spread on the wedding bed. "Mama, I have nothing to do with Tu. We never had sex."

"Are you sure?" Sansan's mother asks, hopeful disbelief in her eyes.

"I'm a spinster losing my mind. If you don't believe me, why don't you ask the town to vote on my virginity?"

Sansan's mother stares at her for a long moment, and claps her hands. "That's even better. I didn't know you loved him so much. I'll go talk to his parents tonight, and tell them you've kept your *cleanness* for him all these years."

"I did nothing for him."

"But why wouldn't you get married, if he never had you?"

Sansan does not reply. She wonders how much of the gossip about her lost virginity burdened her father before his death. She wonders why her mother has never confronted her all these years; but then, how could her mother, a proud yet humble woman of tradition, ask her daughter such a thing when they have never talked about sex in her family?

"If you can't answer the question, it's time to make up your mind," Sansan's mother says.

"My mind has been made up all along. I won't marry Tu."

"Are you going crazy?"

"Mama, why do you want to be the best egg seller in the world?"

Sansan's mother shakes her head. "I don't know what you're talking about." everything for him.

"Mama, why do you put more spices in?"

"If I'm telling people I sell the best eggs in the world, I have to keep my promise."

"But nobody cares about it. You're keeping a promise that matters only to you."

"Don't talk to me like that. I'm an illiterate. Besides, what has that to do with your marriage?"

"I have my own promise to keep."

"Why are you so stubborn? Do you know we'll both end up as crazy women if you don't get married?" Sansan's mother says, and starts to cry.

ANOTHER TRAIN PULLS into the station with a long whistle. Sansan listens to her mother chanting in a trembling voice, and wipes a drop of tear off. Indeed she is going crazy, hurting her mother so, the only person who loves her despite who she is. But she has no other choice. People in this world can discard their promises like used napkins, but she does not want to be one of them.

A man enters the marketplace, in a dirty shirt and jeans and carrying a shapeless bag. He hugs the bag close to his body as if it were a woman. Sansan watches the man sit down at the open space between the two stalls across the aisle from her mother's stove. He takes a flattened cardboard box and a knife out of the bag, the kind with a long and sharp blade that fruit vendors use to cut watermelons. Then he takes off his shirt, points the knife to his left arm, and with a push, carefully slices open his flesh, from the elbow to the shoulder. He seems so calm and measured in his movements that Sansan and a few other people who have noticed him all watch with quiet amazement. The man dips his index finger in the blood, checks his finger as if he is a calligrapher, and writes down the words on the cardboard box: *Give me ten yuan and I will let you slice me once wherever you like; if you finish my life with one cut, you owe me nothing.* WOah

The man has to shout out the words twice before more people gather.

"What a crazy man," an old woman says.

"An inventive way to beg, though," another woman says.

"Why not just begging?"

"Who'd give him money? He's a strong man. He should be able to find some work."

"Young people don't like to work now. They like easy money," an old man says.

"What's easy about hurting oneself?" true

"Hey, what's your story?" a young man asks. "Don't you know you have to make up some really good tragedies to beg?"

People laugh. The man sits quietly in the middle of the circle, the blood dripping from his elbow onto his jeans, but he seems not to notice it. After a while, he shouts the words again.

Sansan's mother sighs. She fumbles in her cash box and then walks to the man. "Here is ten yuan. Take it, young man, and go find a job. Don't waste your life with this nonsense."

"But there's no job to find."

"Take the money then."

The man holds the blade between his two palms, and offers the knife handle to Sansan's mother. "Here you go, Auntie."

"Why? I don't want to cut you."

"But you have to. I can't take your money without you cutting me. It's written here," the man says.

"Just take it."

"I'm not a beggar."

"What are you, then?" someone in the crowd asks.

"An idiot," someone else says, and people break out laughing. The man does not move, still holding out the knife for Sansan's mother. She shakes her head and lets the bill drop onto the cardboard. The man returns the bill to the foot of Sansan's mother, and sits back at his spot.

Sansan picks up the bill and walks to the man. The man looks up at her, and she looks into his eyes. Without a word, he puts the knife in her hand. She studies his body, the naked skin smooth and tanned, and the wound that's quietly bleeding. She touches his upper arm with one finger, testing and calculating, and then moves her fingertip to his shoulder. The man shivers slightly as her finger traces his flesh.

"Sansan, are you crazy?" her mother says.

The man's muscles loosen under her caressing finger; after all these years, she finally meets someone who understands what a promise is. Crazy as they may seem to the world, they are not alone, and they will always find each other. Such is the promise of life; such is the grandeur. "Don't worry, Mama," Sansan says, and turns to smile at her mother before she points the knife at the man's shoulder and slices, slowly opening his flesh with love and tenderness.

this is a lot lol.

integrity >pride. know

Son

HAN, THIRTY-THREE YEARS OLD, SINGLE, SOFT-
ware engineer and recently naturalized American
citizen, arrives at Beijing International Airport with
a brand-new American passport and an old Chinese worry.
He has asked his mother to stay at home; knowing she
would not, he has feared, for the whole flight from San
Francisco to Beijing, that she would be waiting at the terminal with an album of pictures, girls smiling at him out of the
plastic holders, competing to please his eyes and win his
heart. Han is a *zuanshi-wanglaowu,* a diamond bachelor,
earning American dollars and holding American citizenship.
But even when he was at lower levels—silver or gold or
whatever he was—his mother never tired of matchmaking
for him. At first Han said he would not consider marriage
before he got his degree. Then it was a job, and then the
green card. But now that Han has got his American citizenship, he is running out of excuses. He imagines the girls his
mother has collected, all busy weaving sturdy nets to catch
a big fish like him. Han is gay. He has no plan to marry any
one of them, nor does he intend to explain this decision to

his mother. Han loves his mother, but more so he loves himself. He does not want to bring unnecessary pains to his mother's life; he does not want to make any sacrifice out of filial duty, either.

But to his surprise, what his mother presents to him is not a picture album but a gold cross on a gold chain. A miniature of Jesus is pinned to the cross. "I special-ordered it for you," she says. "Feel it."

Han feels the cross, his finger avoiding the crucified figure. The cross is solid and heavy in his hand. "Twenty-four-karat gold," his mother says. "As pure as our faith."

"That sounds like the oath we took when we joined the Communist Youth League. *Our faith in communism is as pure and solid as gold,*" Han says.

"Han, don't make such inappropriate jokes."

"I'm not joking. What I'm saying is that many things are circulated and recycled. Language is one of them. Faith is another one. They are like the bills in our wallets. You can buy anything with them, but they themselves hold no meaning," Han says. His mother tries to smile, but he sees the disappointment she cannot hide. "Sorry, Mama. Of course we can't go on without the paper bills in our wallet."

"You talk a lot now, Han," his mother says.

"I'll shut up then."

"No, it's good you talk more than before. You've always been a quiet child. Baba would be happy to know that you've opened up."

"It's not easy to shut up in America. They value you not by what's inside you, but by what's pouring out of your mouth," Han says.

"Yes, of course," Han's mother says, quickly agreeing. "But Baba would say you have to learn to listen before you open your mouth. Baba would say the more you talk, the less you gain."

"Mama, Baba is dead," Han says. He watches his mother blink and try to find words to fill the vacuum arising between them, and he lets her struggle. For as long as Han remembers, his mother has always been a parrot of his father. The last time Han was on vacation, a few months after his father's death, he was horrified to overhear his mother's conversation with several neighbors. "Han says there's nothing wrong for old people to wear bright colors," his mother said of the red and orange T-shirts he had bought in bulk for his mother and her friends and neighbors. "Han says we should live for our own comforts, not others' opinions." It saddened him back then that his mother had to spend her life repeating her husband's, and then her son's, lines. But his sympathy must have been worn out by the seventeen hours in a crammed jet plane. "Mama, let's get out of here. It's getting late," Han says. He picks up his bags and starts to move toward the revolving glass door.

Han's mother catches up with him and makes a fuss taking over the biggest bag from Han. "Mama, I can handle it myself," Han says.

"But I can't walk empty-handedly with you. I'm your mother."

Han lets go of the bag. They walk silently. Men in suits and women in dresses come up to them, talking to Han about the best hotel deals they have, and Han waves them away. Half a step behind him, his mother apologizes to the hawkers, explaining that they are going home. No, not too far and no need for an overnight place, she says when the hawkers do not give up their hope, and apologizes more.

It upsets Han that his mother is humble for no good

reason. When they reach the end of the line at the taxi station, he says, "Mama, you don't have to apologize to those people."

"But they're trying to help us."

"They only care about the money in your pocket."

"Han." His mother opens her mouth, and then sighs.

"I know—I shouldn't be thinking about people this way, and money is not everything—except it is everything," Han says. He takes out the gold cross he has slipped into his pocket earlier. "Look, even your church encourages you to buy the twenty-four-karat-gold cross. Why? The more you spend on it, the purer your faith is."

Han's mother shakes her head. "Han, come to the church tomorrow with me and listen to our pastor. Ask him about his experience in the Cultural Revolution, and you would know what a great man he is."

"What can he tell me that I don't know?" Han says.

"Don't be so arrogant," his mother says, almost begging.

Han shrugs with exaggeration. They move slowly with the line. After a silent moment, Han asks, "Mama, are you still a member of the Communist Party?"

"No. I sent my membership card back before I was baptized."

"They let you do that! You are not afraid that they'll come back and prosecute you for giving up your communist faith? Remember, Marx, your old god, says religion is the spiritual opium."

Han's mother does not reply. The wind blows her gray hair into her eyes, and she looks despondent. A yellow cab drives in, and Han helps his mother into the backseat. A good son she's got for herself, the cabbie compliments his mother, and she agrees, saying that indeed, he is a very good son.

. . .

LATER THAT NIGHT, unable to sleep from the jet lag, Han slips out of the house and goes to an Internet café nearby. He tries to connect to the several chat rooms where he usually spends his evenings in America, flirting with other men and putting on different personalities for different IDs he owns, but after several failed trials, he realizes that the Internet police have blocked such sites in China. It's daytime in America, and people are busy working anyway. Han sits there for a moment, opening randomly any sites that are available. He feels sorry to have upset his mother earlier, even though she acted as if nothing unpleasant ever happened, and cooked a whole table of dishes for his homecoming. She did not mention the service for tomorrow, and he did not mention the gold cross, which he slipped into his suitcase, ready to forget.

Han is not surprised that his mother has become this devout person. In her letters to him after his father's death, she writes mostly about her newly discovered faith. What bothers Han is that his mother would have never thought of going to the church if his father were still alive. His father wouldn't have allowed anyone, be it a man or a god, to take a slice of her attention away; she wouldn't have had the time for someone else, either, his father always requiring more than she could give. His father's death should be a relief for his mother. She should have started to enjoy her life instead of putting on another set of shackles for herself. Besides, what kind of church does she go to, and what god does she worship, if the whole thing exists in broad daylight in this country? Han remembers reading, in *The New York Times* once, a report about the underground churches in China. He decides to find the article and translate it for his mother.

If she wants to be a Christian, she had better believe in the right god. She needs to know these people, who risk their freedom and lives going to shacks and caves for their faith. Han remembers the pictures from the report, those believers' eyes squinting at the reporter's camera, dispassionate and fearless. Han respects anybody leading an underground life; he himself, being gay, is one of them.

But of course the website of *The New York Times* is blocked, Han realizes a minute later. He searches for the seminaries and organizations referred to in the article, and almost laughs out loud when he finds a report about the Chinese Christian Patriots Association, the official leader of all the state-licensed churches. The association is coordinating several seminars for a national conference, focusing on the role of Christian teachings in the latest theories of communist development in the new millennium. God on the mission to help revive Marxism, Han thinks.

AFTER TWO HOURS of sleep, Han wakes up, and is happy to find the printed article in his pocket, black words on white paper. He walks into his father's study. His mother, sitting at the desk, looks up from behind her bifocals. "Did you have a good sleep?" she asks.

"Yes."

"I've got breakfast ready," his mother says, and puts down a brochure she is reading. Han takes it up, reads a few pages, and tosses it back to his mother's side of the desk. It's a collection of poems written by different generations of believers in mainland China over the past century.

"In your spare time—I know you're busy in America—

but if you have some time to spare, I have some good books for you to read," his mother says.

Han says nothing and goes into the kitchen. He has accepted, in the past ten years, handouts and brochures and several pocket-sized Bibles from people standing in the streets. He lets the young men from the Mormon Church into his kitchen and listens to them for an hour or two. He stands in the parking lots of shopping centers and allows the Korean ladies to preach to him in broken English. He goes to the picnics of the local Chinese church when he is invited, and he does not hang up when people from the church spend a long time trying to convert him. He is never bothered by the inconvenience caused by these people. Once he was stopped outside a fast food restaurant in Cincinnati by a middle-aged woman who insisted on holding both his hands in hers and praying for his soul. He listened and watched a traffic cop write a ticket for his expired meter; even then he did not protest. Han finds it hard to turn away from these people, their concerns for his soul so genuine and urgent that it moves him. Other times, when he sees people standing in the street with handwritten signs that condemn, among many other sinners, homosexuals, he cannot help laughing in their faces. These people, who love or hate him for reasons only good to themselves, amuse Han, but it's because they are irrelevant people, and their passion won't harm him in any way. He imagines his mother being one of them; the mere thought of it irritates him.

She follows him to the kitchen. "You can always start with reading the Bible," she says and puts a steaming bowl of porridge in front of Han. "Purple rice porridge, your favorite."

"Thanks, Mama."

"It's good for you," Han's mother says. Han does not know if she is talking about food, or religion. She sits down on the other side of the table and watches him eat. "I've talked to many people," she says. "Some of them didn't believe me at first, but after they came to the church with me, and read the Bible, their lives were changed."

"My life's good enough. I don't need a change," Han mumbles.

"It's never too late to know the truth. Confucius said: If one gets to know the truth in the morning, he can die in the evening without regret."

"Confucius said: When one reaches fifty, he is no longer deceived by the world. Mama, you are sixty already, and you still let yourself be deceived. Wasn't your communist faith enough of an example?" Han says. "Look here, Mama, I have printed out this lovely message for you. Read it yourself. The church you go to, the god you talk about—it's all made up so people like you can be tricked. Don't you know that all the state-licensed churches recognize the Communist Party as their only leader? Maybe someday you will even come up with the old conclusion that God and Marx are the same."

Han's mother takes the sheet of paper. She seems not surprised, or disappointed. When she finishes reading, she puts the printout carefully in the trash can by the desk, and says, "No cloud will conceal the sunshine forever."

"Mama, I did not come home to listen to you preach. I've been in America for ten years, and enough people have tried to convert me, but I'm sitting here the same person as ten years ago. What does that tell you?"

"But you're my son. I have to help you even if they've failed."

"You could have helped me before. Remember, you

burned my Bible," Han says, and watches her body freeze. He knows that she has forgotten the incident, but he has chosen not to. The Bible was a gift from his best friend when they were thirteen. They were in love without realizing it; innocent boys they were then, their hands never touching. Han did not know what made the boy seek out the Bible, a tightly controlled publication that one could never see in a bookstore or anywhere he knew, as a birthday gift for him. He did not know what trouble the boy had gone through to get the Bible, but he knew, at the time, that it was the most precious gift he had ever got. It would have remained so, well kept and carried along to each city he moved to, a souvenir of the first love, except that his mother made a fire with the Bible and dumped the ashes into the toilet bowl. She did not know the hours he had spent with his best friend after school, sitting together and reading the Bible, finding a haven in the book while their classmates were competing to join the Communist Youth League. They had loved the stories, the bigness of the book that made their worries tiny and transient. When their classmates criticized them for being indifferent to political activities, they laughed it off secretly, both knowing that the Bible allowed them to live in a different, bigger world.

The Bible was discovered by Han's father and then burned by his mother. Afterward, Han was no longer able to face his friend. He made up excuses to stay away from his friend; he found fault with his friend and argued with him for any trivial reason. Their friendship—their love—did not last long afterward. It would have been doomed anyway, a first love that was going nowhere, but the way it ended, someone other than himself was to be blamed. "Remember, it's you who burned the Bible," Han says.

"Yes," his mother says, trying hard to find words. "But Baba said it was not appropriate to keep it. It was a different time then."

"Yes, a different time then because it was Baba who gave out orders, and it was the communist god you both worshipped. And now Baba is gone, and you've got yourself a new god to please," Han says. "Mama, why can't you use your own brain to think?"

"I'm learning, Han. This is the first decision that I've made on my own."

A wrong decision it is, but Han only smiles out of pity and tolerance.

LATER, WHEN HIS mother cautiously suggests a visit to the church, Han says he will accompany her for the bus ride. It won't hurt to go in and listen, his mother says, but Han only nods noncommittally.

West Hall, the church that Han used to ride his bicycle past on his way to high school years ago, remains the same gray nondescript building inside the rusty iron fence, but the alleys around were demolished, and the church, once a prominent landmark of the area, is now dwarfed by the surrounding shopping centers. Han watches people of all ages enter the church, nodding at one another politely. He wonders how much these people understand of their placing their faiths in the wrong hands, and how much they care about it.

A few steps away from the entrance, Han's mother stops. "Are you coming in with me?" she asks.

"No, I'll sit in the Starbucks and wait for you."

"Starbucks?"

"The coffee shop over there."

Han's mother stretches and looks at it, no doubt the first time she has noticed its existence. She nods without moving. "Mama, go in now," Han says.

"Ah, yes, just a moment," she says and looks around with expectation. Soon two little beggars, a boy and a girl, run across the street to her. Brother and sister they seem to be, both dressed up in rags, their hands and faces smeared with dirt and soot. The boy, seven or eight years old, holds out a hand when he sees Han. "Uncle, spare a penny. Our baba died with a large debt. Our mama is sick. Spare a penny, please. We need money to send our mama to the hospital."

The girl, a few years younger, follows suit and chants the same lines. Han looks at the boy. There is a sly expression in the boy's eyes that makes Han uncomfortable. He knows they are children employed for the begging job, if not by their parents, then by relatives or neighbors. The adults, older and less capable of moving people with their tragedies, must be monitoring the kids from not far away. Han shakes his head. He does not have one penny for such kids; on his previous vacations, he even fought with the kids, who grabbed his legs tightly and threatened not to loose their grip until they were paid. Han is not a stingy person. In America he gives away dollar bills to the musicians playing in the street, quarters and smaller change for homeless people who sit at the same spot all day long. They are honest workers according to Han's standard, and he gives them what they deserve. But child laborers are not acceptable, and people using the children deserve nothing. Han pushes the boy's hand away, and says, "Leave me alone."

"Don't bother Uncle," Han's mother says to the children, and they both stop chanting right away. Han's mother takes out two large bills from her purse, and gives one to each child. "Now come with Granny," she says. The children carefully put the money away and follow Han's mother to the church entrance.

"Wait a minute, Mama," Han says. "You pay them every week to go to church with you?"

"It can only benefit them," Han's mother says.

"But this is not right."

"It doesn't hurt anyone. They would have to beg in the street otherwise."

"It hurts my principles," Han says. He takes out several bills from his wallet and says to the boy, "Now listen. I will pay you double the amount if both of you return the money to her and do not go to the church today."

"Han!"

"Hold it, Mama. Don't say a word," Han says. He squats down and flips the bills in front of the children's eyes. The girl looks up at the boy, and the boy looks up at Han's mother for a moment and then looks down at the money. The cunning and the calculation in the boy's eyes infuriate Han; he imagines his mother deceived even by such small children. "Come on," he says to the boy, still smiling. A few seconds later, the boy accepts Han's money and gathers the bill from his sister's hand and returns the two bills to Han's mother. "Good," Han says. "You can go now."

The children walk away, stopping people in the sidewalk and repeating their begging lines. Han turns to his mother with a smile. "What did this tell you, Mama? The only thing that matters to them is money."

"Why did you do that?" his mother says.

"I need to protect you."

"I don't need your protection," Han's mother says.

"You can say that, Mama," Han says. "But the truth is, I'm protecting you, and it's my duty to do this."

"What right do you have to talk about the truth?" his mother says, and turns away for the church.

HAN TRIES TO convince himself that he is not upset by his mother's words. Still, he feels hurt. He is his mother's son. The boy who accepted the money from him is a son, too, but someday he will become a husband, a father, maybe sending his sons and daughters into the street to beg, maybe giving them a better life. Han will never become a father—he imagines himself known to the world only as someone's son. Not many men would remain only as sons all their lives, but Jesus is one. It's not easy being a son with duties, Han thinks, and smiles bitterly to himself. What right does he have? His right is that he lives with his principles. He works. He got laid off, struggled for a few months, but found work again. He pays his rent. He greets his neighbors. He goes to the gym. He watches news channels but not reality shows. He sponsors a young girl's education in a rural province in China, sending checks regularly for her tuition and her living expenses. He masturbates, but not too often. He does not believe in long-term relationships, but once in a while, he meets men in local bars, enjoys physical pleasure with them, and uses condoms. He flirts with other men, faceless as he himself is, on the Internet, but he makes sure they talk about arts too. He loves his mother. He sends two thousand dollars to her every year, even though she has said many times that she does not need the money. He sends the money still, because he is her son, and it's his duty to protect her and nurture her, as she protected and nurtured him in his younger years. He saves up his vacation and goes home to spend time with her, but what happens when they are together? A day into the vacation and they are already hurting each other.

Han walks across the street to the Starbucks. He feels tired and sad, but then it is his mother's mistake, not his, that makes them unhappy, and he decides to forgive her. A few steps away from the coffee shop, there is a loud squealing noise of tires on the cement road. Han turns and looks. Men and women are running toward a car, where a crowd has already gathered. A traffic accident, people are yelling, a kid run over. More people swarm toward the accident, some dialing the emergency number on their cellphones, others calling their friends and family, reporting a traffic accident they are witnessing, gesturing as they speak, full of excitement. A man dressed in old clothes runs toward the crowd. "My child," he screams.

Han freezes, and then starts walking again, away from the accident. He does not want to see the man, who must have been smoking in a shaded corner a block or two away, cry now like a bereaved parent. He does not want to know if it's the young girl with the singsong voice, or her brother with the sly smile in his eyes, that was run over. Traffic accidents happen every day in this city. People pay others to take their driving tests for them or buy their driver's licenses directly from the black market; cars do not yield to pedestrians, pedestrians do not fear the moving vehicles. If he does not look, it could be any child, a son, a daughter, someone irrelevant and forgettable.

But somehow, Han knows it's the boy. It has to be the boy, ready to deceive anyone who is willing to be deceived. The boy will remain a son and never become a father. He will be forgotten by the crowd once his blood is rinsed clean from the ground; his sister will think of him but soon she will forget him, too. He will live on only in Han's memory, a child punished not for his own insincerity but someone else's disbelief.

Han sits in Starbucks by the window and waits for his mother. When she finally walks out of the church, the street is cleared and cleaned, not a trace of the accident left. Han walks out to meet his mother, his hands shaking. Across the street she smiles at him, hope and love in her eyes, and Han knows she has already forgotten the unpleasant incident from two hours earlier. She will always forgive him because he is her son. She will not give up her effort to save his soul because he is her son. But he does not want to be forgiven, or saved. He waits until his mother safely arrives at his side of the street, and says without looking at her, "Mama, there is something I want you to know. I'll never get married. I only like men."

Han's mother does not speak. He smiles and says, "A shock, right? What would Baba say if he knew this? Disgusting, isn't it?"

After a long moment, Han's mother says, "I've guessed. That's why I didn't try matchmaking for you this time."

"So you see, I'm doomed," Han says. "I'm one of those— what did we say of those counterrevolutionaries back then?—stinky and hard and untransformable as a rock in an outhouse pit."

"I wouldn't say so," Han's mother says.

"Admit it, Mama. I'm doomed. Whoever your god is, he wouldn't be fond of people like me."

"You're wrong," Han's mother says. She stands on tiptoe and touches his head, the way she used to touch his head when he was younger, to reassure him that he was still a good boy even after he did something wrong. "God loves you for who you are, not what others expect you to be," she says. "God sees everything, and understands everything."

Of course, Han wants to make a joke. Her god is just like a Chinese parent, never running out of excuses to love a son. But he stays quiet when he looks up at his mother, her eyes so eager and hopeful that he has to avert his own.

The Arrangement

UNCLE BING CAME TO VISIT RUOLAN AND HER mother when her father went away on business trips. Ruolan's father worked as a salesman for a tea factory, so every year in late spring, he traveled with samples of new tea to Shanghai, Nanjing, Beijing, big cities Ruolan dreamed of visiting when she grew up. Earlier on, he had come home before summer, but each year he traveled longer, and by the time Ruolan was ten years old, he did not show up until late December, when he was home just in time for the end-of-the-year housecleaning and the holidays. He sent postcards but not often. He brought Ruolan gifts from the cities, too: a doll with blond, curly hair and blue, deep-set eyes, fragrant rubber erasers in the shapes of little bunnies, dresses with laces and shining decorations that were too fancy for the town. Her mother put the dresses away in a trunk and never let Ruolan touch them. After a while, she learned not to ask. She wore passed-down clothes of her mother's to school, gray blouses and blue pants, faded and too big. *Gray-Skinned Mouse,* the boys in school nicknamed Ruolan, but even that had stopped bothering her.

Uncle Bing lived in the mountains nearby, and was the only teacher in the small village school there. He was not married. He was not even a relative, but as long as Ruolan remembered, he had been Uncle Bing. Every spring, before her father's trip, he left an envelope for Ruolan; inside were a piece of paper with Uncle Bing's address and enough money for the round-trip bus fare. "Go find Uncle Bing in case of an emergency," Ruolan's father told her. She had never taken the trip once; there was no need really, as Uncle Bing came to visit Ruolan and her mother every weekend when her father went away. The paper bills Ruolan had put away, between pages of an old textbook that she hid under her straw mattress.

On Saturday evenings, Uncle Bing arrived, with a small basket of bayberries, or apricots, or freshly picked edible ferns, gifts from the students and their parents. They cost Uncle Bing nothing, but Ruolan's mother always thanked him as if he had gone to great trouble to get them. "It's so very kind of you, Uncle Bing. How could we ever repay you for your generosity?" she said.

Ruolan frowned. Her mother had the ability to fill her words, even the best-meaning ones, with disdain and sarcasm. Uncle Bing, however, was not annoyed. He went into the yard to chop the firewood, and when he became warm, he took off his shirt and hung it over the clothesline. From the kitchen, where Ruolan was cooking, she looked at the small and big holes in his undershirt. When she had been small, she used to stick her fingers into the holes and call it a fishnet. She no longer did it now; thirteen years old she was, and already she had started missing her childhood, when she had been less restrained around Uncle Bing, and happier.

Uncle Bing went on to fix the grapevine trellis that had been partly taken down by an early storm. Ruolan watched him work, and cut the vegetables halfheartedly until her mother called from the bedroom, "Does the knife weigh a thousand tons?"

Ruolan did not answer and chopped the celery with an angry speed.

At supper, Ruolan's mother poured the strong yam wine for Uncle Bing. They talked about the weather, too much rain or too little, and how the peasants' lives would be affected, even though neither of them needed to worry about the harvest season. Ruolan listened to their pointless chatting and spun the chopsticks between her fingers. Her mother did not tell her to stop the bad-mannered game in a snapping voice when Uncle Bing was around.

Sometimes, when they ran out of small talk, Uncle Bing poured a cup of yam wine for Ruolan's mother, and they let the rims of the cups touch slightly. She took a few sips, which made her cough and blush, and she would tell Ruolan to see to it that Uncle Bing had a good drink, and then excuse herself and retreat to the bedroom.

"How's Mama's health?" Uncle Bing asked Ruolan after her mother left.

Ruolan shrugged and did not reply. Her mother had been ill, or thought of herself as ill, for as long as Ruolan remembered. Every morning, her mother rocked her awake and told her to get rid of the dregs from the medicine pot—it was said that to make a patient recover, the dregs were to be scattered on the crossroads for people to trample on. Ruolan believed that her mother did it only to remind the world that she herself was not well; since age five, Ruolan had been the one to carry the medicine pot into town, disgusted by the bitter smell of the leftover herbs, her mother's prolonged and fake illness, and the looks people gave her.

Uncle Bing drank silently for a few cups. Ruolan pushed a plate of fried peanuts toward him. "Uncle Bing, drink slowly," she said.

He downed another cup. "Want to hear a story, Ruolan? Once upon a time, there was a man who loved dragons so dearly he had dragons painted everywhere in his mansion."

"And when the real dragon came to visit him, he was scared out of his wits," Ruolan said. "You've told it many times before."

"Once upon a time there was a man who spent a fortune to buy a pearl—"

"And he fell in love with the box, and thought it alone was worthy of the money, so he returned the pearl to the seller," Ruolan said. "Why are your stories always about idiots?"

Uncle Bing smiled a sad and drunk smile. "What other stories can an idiot tell?"

Ruolan regretted her impatience right away. It had always been a game between them that Uncle Bing told stories and sang folk tunes to her when they were left alone. But she knew enough now to start suspecting the real reason for those stories and songs. The neighborhood grannies and aunties commented to her on her father's long absence, and the frequent visits of Uncle Bing. "Do they send you to bed early?" some of them asked, their smiles pregnant with mean curiosity. "Is your mother still sick when your uncle's around?"

Ruolan tried to ignore the women, chatty and shameless like a group of female ducks, but they had left something poisonous inside her. She had looked at herself in the mirror and tried to find a resemblance to her father's face, or Uncle Bing's. She did not look like either of them.

"Here's a new story," Uncle Bing said and poured another cup for himself. "Once upon a time a man heard the story about magic leaves. If you put a magic leaf in front of your eyes, it would make you disappear so nobody would be able to see you. The man believed in the story, and went out to gather bags of leaves every day. He put each leaf in front of his eyes and asked his wife, 'Can you see me now?' The wife said yes until she finally lost her patience. 'Oh, heaven, where are you, my husband? I can't see you now.' The man was happy. 'Finally, the magic leaf!' he said, and went to the marketplace with the leaf in front of his eyes. But when he tried to steal, people caught him and gave him a good beating."

Ruolan laughed for the sake of Uncle Bing. He laughed, too. "Poor woman. How could she marry such a stupid man?" Ruolan said afterward.

"Perhaps her father didn't pay the matchmaker enough," Uncle Bing said.

"Perhaps she was very ugly, she could only marry an idiot."

"Or she was a lazy woman, nobody else wanted to marry her."

"Or when she was a girl, she *stole men,* so only an idiot wouldn't mind being a cuckold," Ruolan said with a wicked joy.

"Don't say words that you don't understand," Uncle Bing said.

"I'm not a child anymore," she said. "A good woman doesn't let her husband live elsewhere and let another man visit her every week."

"Ruolan," Uncle Bing said, and she stared back until he looked away. "You're a big girl now, and Uncle Bing is old," he said, and got up drunkenly.

Ruolan ran across the room and made a bed for him in her cot before he could stop her. When Uncle Bing came and stayed overnight, he slept in her cot at the corner of the living room, and she slept with her mother in her big bed. "Uncle Bing," she said, the edge of her defiance softened by a sudden pity for his sadness, "have a nice sleep."

Later, Ruolan huddled on the edge of the bed, as far away as possible from her mother, whose shallow and quick breathing reminded Ruolan of a dying fish. Ruolan covered her head with the blanket, but the smell of her own body, warm and familiar, mixed with the bitterness of the herbs from her mother's bed, nauseated her. She wished she would never have to sleep near her mother, but then, when Uncle Bing's bus was late, she was the one to look out the door for the sight of him every three minutes until her mother reminded her not to lean on to the door frame like a shameless girl displaying herself for all the men in the world.

Every time after Uncle Bing left, Ruolan buried her head in her pillow and sniffed the unfamiliar scent of his hair. It smelled strangely comforting, different from the stinky boys in her class, or her own home.

ON THE FIRST day of every month, Ruolan walked to the cement factory three miles outside the town for the illness allowance for her mother. Ruolan's mother had stopped working totally two years ago. She was forty-one now, still four years short for the early retirement pension.

Ruolan signed the slip and accepted the few bills, soft and worn out, from the old accountant. "How's your mother?" he asked.

"All right."

The old man looked at Ruolan from above his glasses and shook his head. *"The most beautiful woman always has the saddest fate,"* he said. "When your mother first came—you were a baby then—she looked so young that you'd think she was only sixteen. Who'd imagine that she would become ill so early?"

Ruolan left the old man lost in his own sentiment. She could not imagine her mother possessing any beauty. Because she lay in bed all day long, her complexion was sickly pale, almost translucent. Her hair, carelessly cut by herself, was like a bird's nest most of the time. She wore her pajamas even when she had to walk to the next lane for the public outhouse. On Saturday afternoons, however, before Uncle Bing's arrival, she cleaned herself and changed into her best clothes. She powdered her face, too, with stale, caked rouge; it gave her hollowed cheeks an unnatural pink, as if she were a patient dying from consumption.

That summer, Ruolan had her first period. She was not surprised; she had seen darkly stained tissues in the public outhouse, and had heard other girls her age discuss it. She found an old cotton shirt in a trunk and ripped it into rags. "What are you making all the noises for? I'm having a headache now," her mother said from her bed.

Ruolan hesitated and answered, "I have my *bad luck* with me."

Her mother sighed aloud and came out to the living room. *"Bad luck?* What's bad about it?"

"What do you call it, then, Mama?" Ruolan said. Her mother had never talked about it with her; moreover, untidy as her mother was, Ruolan had never seen stained underwear or any sign of her having the monthly visit of her *bad luck.*

"It's not something you need a name for," Ruolan's mother snapped. "You don't need to go around and talk to everybody about it."

"Whatever," Ruolan said under her breath.

Ruolan's mother stared at Ruolan with contempt. "Why does a patient want to waste her energy talking to a brat like you?" her mother said, and counted a few bills and coins from her small silk purse. "Go buy what you need."

Ruolan accepted the money. She did not know what she needed, but she would rather ask a stranger in the street than her own mother.

"And stop by at the old pharmacy," her mother said, and brought out a piece of carbon paper and two more bills. "Ask for a week's dose for yourself."

Ruolan looked at her mother's handwriting on the paper. It was the same prescription her mother sent her to fill every month, the mixture of grass roots, tree barks, and dried flowers that her mother boiled the first thing in the morning. "I'm not sick," Ruolan said.

"A prolonged illness makes a good doctor out of a patient," her mother said. "I know what you need."

"I've heard that all medicines are poisons," Ruolan said.

"Are you saying that your mother wants to poison you?"

"I'm only saying maybe it's not good for you, or anyone, to have medicine every day."

"I'm ill," her mother said. She dropped the bill and the carbon paper on Ruolan's cot. "You're a woman now, so you'd better listen to me," her mother said. "Being a woman is itself an illness."

Before Ruolan replied, her mother walked back to her bedroom. Ruolan looked at her mother's feet, skinny and ashen colored in the tattered, sky blue slippers. She felt choked by disgust and pity for her mother's body. Her own body had changed over the last two months, her breasts swelling with a strange, painful itch. She imagined herself growing into a woman like her mother; it was the last thing she wanted from life. She squeezed the carbon paper into a small ball and flipped it through the open door to the courtyard. She flattened the extra bills with her palm and put them in her textbook.

Ruolan's father came home the next week, much too early. For the first time, Ruolan was overjoyed to see him. They had never been close. She had got used to his absence, and now she understood the reason for it. They were comrades, trapped in a life with the woman they could not love, but could not leave, either.

At the end of the dinner that evening, Ruolan's father brought up the topic of a divorce. He had submitted an application to his and her working units, he said. In a few days they would expect the welfare officials from both factories to come and dissuade them, but if they could agree on the divorce, the officials would sign the application so they could go to the county courthouse to replace their marriage certificate with a divorce certificate.

Ruolan's mother did not reply. She dipped the head of a chopstick in the soup and drew linked circles on the table. Her father's eyes followed the strokes of the chopstick. He looked older than Ruolan remembered; his hair, at forty-five, was more gray than black.

"What if I don't agree?" her mother said finally.

"We'll have to go to the court," her father looked at his own palms and said. "But why do we have to make it hard for us?"

"For you, you mean? Why should I agree to save you the disgrace of going into the court?" Ruolan's mother said. "You're the one to keep a mistress."

Her father looked at Ruolan and said, "Go out and play, Ruolan."

"Let her stay. She's a woman now. She should learn from my lesson of how to keep a man."

It was not about keeping a man; it was a lesson on how not to become an ugly woman. Ruolan felt a revenging joy of seeing her father leave her mother. She was ready to desert her, too.

Ruolan's father opened his mouth, but before he could say anything, her mother cut him off. "Don't say anything. I won't agree to sign," she said, and stood up. "I won't let you off the hook so easily," she said before she banged the bedroom door closed. The venom in her words made Ruolan shudder. She looked at her father, tired and crestfallen, his lips quavering. "Baba," she said in a low voice, "are you going to take me in after the divorce?"

"I'm sorry, but Mama needs you more than I do," Ruolan's father said, still studying his palms. "She's ill."

"I'm not her medicine," Ruolan said, choked with disappointment in her father.

He looked up at her, but his eyes were empty, his mind already floating to another place. "Am I your daughter, Baba?" Ruolan asked.

Her father looked at her for a long moment and said, "No."

"Am I Uncle Bing's daughter?"

"No," her father said, and picked up the suitcase that he had not unpacked. "You're your mother's daughter," he said, and ran away into the night street before she could ask more questions.

The next morning, Ruolan's mother did not wake her for the medicine pot, and Ruolan got up late for school. The door to her mother's bedroom was closed. For a moment, Ruolan imagined her mother hanged from the ceiling with a broken neck and a long, dangling tongue. She shivered and pushed the door; it was bolted from inside. "Mama," she said. When there was no reply, she hit the door with a fist and started to cry.

After a while, her mother opened the door. "What are you wailing for the first thing in the morning?" she said and shoveled the medicine pot into Ruolan's hands. "You think I would kill myself and let your father get away so easily?"

Ruolan wiped her tears dry. Halfway to the crossroads, she changed her mind and walked back. Her mother's bedroom door was closed, and Ruolan dumped the dregs by the door. She unloaded all her books onto her cot and put her clothes, a few pieces altogether, into her book bag. She took the old textbook from underneath her mattress and counted the bills, enough for a day and a night of bus ride to Shanghai, she imagined; but when she reached the ticket window at the bus station, she lost her courage and asked only for a ticket to Uncle Bing's village.

TWO HOURS LATER, Ruolan got off the bus, and, after getting lost a few times, she found the mud shack that served as the classroom for the village school. About twenty boys and girls, of all grades, sat on wooden benches, reading together a story about a tadpole looking for his mother. Uncle Bing was walking around, patting the younger kids' heads while reading along with them.

Ruolan walked away before Uncle Bing saw her. Across the yard there was a smaller shack. She pushed the door ajar and entered. It was dark inside and it took her a few seconds to see the cot and the desk covered with workbooks and papers. At one corner of the shack was a stove, on which a huge pot of millet porridge was simmering. Ruolan sat down on the stool in front of the stove, and out of habit she took up the ladle and stirred the porridge. The handle of the ladle had been broken and fixed with a pair of chopsticks bound together. She stroked the chopsticks with a finger, and imagined living her life in this shack, cooking for Uncle Bing, waiting for him to finish work, loving him like a good woman.

The door opened and Uncle Bing came in. Ruolan saw his expression change from surprise to worriment. "Is there something wrong?" he said, and clutched Ruolan's shoulder. "Is Mama all right?"

"She's fine," Ruolan said.

"Ah, Ruolan. You've scared the soul out of me," Uncle Bing said and let go of her. "Why are you not in school today?"

"Uncle Bing, the porridge is ready," Ruolan said.

"Ah, yes," he said. "Let me get it to the students first. They must be hungry now."

"Do you cook for the students?"

"Otherwise I wouldn't have more than half of them," Uncle Bing said, and explained that for many students, the porridge would be their only meal during the day, and they came to school because of that.

"Baba came home yesterday and asked for a divorce from Mama," Ruolan said, cutting off Uncle Bing.

"So he told me. He came by last night," Uncle Bing said, and went out of the shack with the porridge. Ruolan sat down on the cot and looked at the pillowcase, torn at a corner and in need also of a good wash. She remembered Uncle Bing's scent left on her pillow.

When Uncle Bing came back with the empty pot, Ruolan had found the sewing bag in a basket underneath the cot, and was mending the pillowcase. The needle was rusted, and she wiped it on her hair from time to time. Uncle Bing watched her work for a moment and then said that he had canceled the afternoon's class. Ruolan looked out the window and saw the children chase one another off. "Let's catch the next bus home," Uncle Bing said and walked to the door. "Mama must need comfort now."

Ruolan checked the stitches without replying. He had only one person in his heart, and Ruolan was disappointed that it was not she. "Don't worry," she said finally. "Mama won't die before everyone she knows dies first."

"Ruolan," Uncle Bing said disapprovingly. "She's your mother."

"Is she really?" Ruolan said, looking up at Uncle Bing. "Baba said I wasn't his daughter. How could I be her daughter?"

"She brought you up."

"She did it only to have someone to torment."

"Ruolan." Uncle Bing raised his voice, and she stared back. "She's in a bad mood because she's ill. You need to help her feel better," he said.

Ruolan did not reply, and started sewing again. When she finished, she broke the thread between her teeth and ran a finger to smooth the stitches. She patted the pillow into a good shape before putting it back on the bed. "Why do people all expect me to be her medicine?" she asked.

Uncle Bing sat down by the stove. "You're the only one she has now," he said.

Ruolan sneered. Uncle Bing hesitated, and said, "Perhaps it's time to know their story so you'll understand her."

"There's nothing for me to understand," Ruolan said.

Uncle Bing ignored her words. He poured a bowl of water into the stove to put out the leftover fire, and said, "I've known your mother all my life, since when we were small children. She was a beautiful girl. She was loved by many boys my age, and she was proud and happy about it, but when we reached eighteen, something changed. The proposals that many of us sent with the matchmakers to her parents were rejected, and she became less happy. Her parents must be holding on to her for an offer better than any of us could afford, the townspeople said; look how the greedy parents are wasting her youth for money, the townspeople said. Soon many boys found other girls as wives, but year after year, there was no sign of marriage on her side. They must have some unspeakable and dirty secret in the family, the townspeople said, and then had wild guesses. Your mother became very sad and pale.

"The year when we were twenty-seven, her parents suddenly married her off to your father, who lived two counties away. After the wedding, the couple moved to a new town even farther away. I was the only boy who hadn't married then. A fool stricken by love, people said about me, and perhaps I was. When she left, I moved too, to the town where she lived with her husband. I thought I would be satisfied if only I could see her in the street from time to time; but a few days after the wedding, rumors started that every night the bridegroom was heard sobbing in the yard. People talked about the scandal that the bridegroom's family must have hid his mental disorder from the bride before the wedding, and when your mother's family did not show up to denounce the cheating, people looked down upon her, too.

"For the first year of their marriage, I was your mother's only friend, and she came to talk to me every day, until there were rumors about our affair. I thought it would only make her life more miserable, so I planned to leave her for good. When your father learned that I was leaving, he came to visit me. I thought he was coming to fight me; I told him your mother and I were innocent, but he only smiled and brought out a bottle of liquor. We drank for the whole night like a pair of old friends, and he told me his story. He had been in love with a widow twelve years his senior since he was fifteen, he said. His family thought a wife would cure him of his infatuation with the older woman, so they arranged for him to marry a girl from out of town and arranged for them to move away so nobody would know his history. But on the wedding night, your mother told him that she could not become his real wife."

"Why?" Ruolan said for the first time since Uncle Bing started the story.

Uncle Bing hesitated for a moment, and said, "Your mother—she is a *stone woman*."

"A *stone woman*?"

"It's something you'll understand when you're older," Uncle Bing said.

"How does one know if she's a stone woman?" Ruolan asked. She wondered if all the medicine her mother drank in the morning year after year had turned her into a solid rock.

Ruolan wondered if she herself would be poisoned, by the years of breathing in the bitterness from the dregs, into an ugly and cold woman like her mother.

Uncle Bing did not reply, his eyes looking past Ruolan into a distant past. "She told your father to either live with the fact or divorce her; she said she didn't mind because her only goal was to get married and leave her hometown so people would no longer talk about her. Your father was shocked that her family had cheated in the matchmaking, but he could not tell this to anyone, including his family. I asked him why, and he said a husband was a husband no matter what was missing from the marriage, and it would be unforgivable if he attacked his wife's name even with the truth. Besides, he said, they deserved it because they had planned to deceive, too. Your father, he's one of the good people in the world. There was nothing wrong with his mind. He was in love with an older woman, that's all, but he was willing to be thought a crazy person and stay in the marriage to protect your mother's name.

"After that night, your father and I became close friends. I helped them to adopt you. We—your father and I— thought it would make their marriage better if they could raise a child together. To make you their own child, they moved farther away, to a different province—where we live now—so that people would not know anything about their past. I did not move at first; I thought I would let them live in their own marriage, and it seemed that things were fine for a while. But after three years, your father came to visit me again. We had another night of drinking, and he confessed that he could not help going back to the widow from time to time. Your mother was very upset when she found out about it, and she refused to leave her bed. I moved again to be close to your mother. I came to take care of her and you when your father was away to live with the other woman. He stuck to his words and came home as a husband for the year-end housecleaning and celebration. The rest of the story you've known. Believe me, Ruolan, your parents are good people. They've tried all these years; they've tried very hard."

"Why does he want a divorce now?"

"The other woman—she used to work as a nanny for people—she's sick now, and he wants to marry her so he can take care of her, and help with the medical bills."

Ruolan thought about her father and the other woman, and she pitied them. "Why didn't you get married, Uncle Bing?" she said.

Uncle Bing smiled. "I'm one of those fools who puts a magic leaf in front of his eyes and then stops seeing mountains and seas."

"Would you marry Mama if their divorce goes through?"

"What difference would a marriage make now?" he said.

Ruolan was relieved but unsatisfied. "Don't marry her," she said. "She's poisonous. Look how she's already destroyed half of a life for Baba. You don't want her to destroy your whole life."

"Ruolan!" Uncle Bing raised his voice.

Ruolan looked at the dark veins on his forehead. He looked unfamiliar, ferocious even, but she did not recoil. She had seen two men poisoned into sad and sheepish beings by her mother, and she wanted to correct the mistake. "What's good about her? She's lazy, ugly, bad-tempered," Ruolan said. "Whatever she does, I can do a hundred times better."

"Ruolan?"

"Think about it, Uncle Bing. We're not related to her. We can leave her, and make a new family ourselves. I can cook. I can sew. I'll do all the housework. I'll find a job after middle school. When you are too old to work, I'll earn money and support you. Why do you need her if you have me?"

Uncle Bing watched her with a sad, tender look. "You're too young to know what you're talking about," he said.

"I'm old enough to tell what's good for you," Ruolan said, and felt something soften inside her. She was not a *stone woman*, after all. She walked to where Uncle Bing sat on the stool, bent down, and put her hands palms down on his knees. "Uncle Bing," she said in a whisper, looking into his eyes the way she imagined a seductive woman would do. "Have you heard of the saying that what a mother owes, a daughter pays back?"

Uncle Bing's lips quavered. "No, I've never heard it."

"Now you know," Ruolan said, and touched Uncle Bing's face, his sideburns stubby under her palm. Uncle Bing breathed hard, and then brushed her hand off gently. "Your mother doesn't owe me," he said, putting his head between his hands, not looking at her.

Ruolan knelt down and looked up at Uncle Bing. "You need an antidote for her poison," she said eagerly. "Baba has his other woman. You need one yourself, too."

"You're a big girl now, and Uncle Bing is getting old," he said. "It's getting late. Why don't you catch the next bus home so Mama doesn't worry about you?"

Ruolan burst into tears. "Why don't you understand me?" she said.

"I do," Uncle Bing said. "But let's keep life as it is."

"What's good about this life, Uncle Bing?"

"You and Mama are my only family now. I can't afford losing either one of you."

Ruolan wiped the tears with the back of her hands. She stared at Uncle Bing; he looked weak, despondent, beaten, and she pitied him. If she was willing, she could keep the nameless love, not of a daughter or of a lover, but both. She could as well stay in the arrangement, tolerating her mother for his sake, but then, why should she choose misery because of love? Why should she choose misery for any reason? She touched the money in her pocket. "I'm leaving, Uncle Bing," Ruolan said, and tears rolled down her cheeks. Perhaps when she was gone, he would realize what a mistake he had made; perhaps only then she would beat her mother, and he would understand that he had chosen the wrong woman.

"Tell Mama I'll come Saturday," Uncle Bing said, still not daring to look up at Ruolan.

Death Is Not a Bad Joke
If Told the Right Way

THE HOUSE OF MR. AND MRS. PANG IS THE PLACE where I can take a break from being someone's daughter. The days spent there, one summer week and one winter week, are the only time when I am not living under my schoolteacher mother. Being someone's child is a difficult job, a position one has no right to quit. Heaven forgive every child who dreams of being an orphan while her parents are working with backs bent to make the child's life a happy one. No life seems happier than an orphan's life for a non-orphan like me. So many times have I dreamed of standing on a street corner, wearing shabby clothes two sizes too small, my ankles and wrists frozen to a bluish white. In my dream I am singing songs about all the sadness in the world, my small voice quavering in the wind. After the most heartbreaking song, I bow to the crowd and they let streams of coins drop into my street singer's basket, men sighing and women wiping tears away with their fingertips.

"Good singing. Sing another song, Little Blossom." It is always the sons of Mr. and Mrs. Song who clap and awaken me from my daydreaming. I am standing in the center of Mrs. Pang's yard, wearing my brand-new bunny coat, snow white fur soft and smooth, the two long ears too tender to stay up, resting on my forehead like extra bangs. I push the ears aside and blush from excitement. Little Blossom is not my name but the name of a famous heroine in a movie, played by my favorite actress, Chen Chong. At sixteen, she is already the most famous actress in the country; every day she smiles at me from the calendar by my bedside.

"Come on," the oldest of the four boys says. "Do you want to be a *little blossom*?"

I nod hard and the two ears flap in front of my eyes. In other dreams, always following the dreams of being an orphan selling her singing voice, I would eventually grow up into an actress like Chen Chong, my beautiful face on other people's walls, wearing makeup. Only actresses are allowed to wear makeup without being denounced as morally degenerate. Lipstick and rouge are part of my orphan dreams.

"Oh yeah, you want to be a little blossom for us?" the second of the four brothers says with a teasing smile. The four boys roar in laughter. At seven years old I am too young to understand the meaning of the little blossom in their vocabulary. I laugh with them but Mrs. Pang stops me. She rushes out from the kitchen and waves a spatula at the boys. "Watch your mouths," she says. The boys laugh again and go back to their room. Mrs. Pang drags me out of the yard and puts me down on the female stone lion in front of the quadrangle. The heads of the pair of lions were chopped off by the Red Guards during the Cultural Revolution as part of the old trash. I sit astride the lioness, fingering the sharp edges left by the axes.

"Now, don't get mixed up with the Song boys," Mrs. Pang said. "Wait here. We are going to the market soon."

Mrs. Pang does not like the Song family. Mr. and Mrs.

Song started as tenants, renting the room at the western side of the quadrangle, but they stopped paying when Mr. Pang was kicked out of his working unit as an enemy of the People. Mr. and Mrs. Song stayed, claiming themselves to be the legal owners of the room. During the years of their occupancy, they demolished Mr. Pang's flower bed and built a kitchen on the spot. They installed clotheslines between Mr. Pang's pomegranate tree and grape trellis, their flagging underwear the permanent decoration of the yard. They produced four sons, and the six of them are still living in one room, the youngest son already sixteen and the oldest twenty-three.

THE MORNING SUN is halfway up in the sky. Three old men are sitting under the north wall of the alley, their eyes closed and their toothless mouths half open, enjoying this unusually warm winter day in Beijing. On the other side of the alley, four girls are jumping rope, chanting a song I have never heard before: "*One two three four five. Let's go hunt the tiger. The tiger does not eat man. The tiger only eats Truman.*" It will be years later when I realize that the Truman they are singing about was the American president during the Korean War, so in the winter of 1979, the song makes little sense to me. I sit there and chant the song silently to myself. After a while the four girls stop singing and start to draw squares on the ground. I jump down from the lion. "Can I join you?" I ask.

"Say the pledge," a girl says and the four of them quickly surround me hand in hand, waiting solemnly.

"What pledge?" I ask.

"You don't know the pledge?" a girl says, making a face. "Where are you from? The Java Island?"

"No, I am from the Institute."

"What institute?" the girl says.

"Let's not waste time," another girl cuts in. "Say with me: *I promise to Chairman Mao—she who does not obey the rule is Liu Shaoqi.*"

"Who is Liu Shaoqi?"

"A counterrevolutionary," the girl says, impatient with my ignorance.

I take the oath, feeling strange that they have so many rules unknown to me. It will also be years later when I know more about Liu Shaoqi: a loyal follower and close colleague of Chairman Mao, he was tortured to death by a group of teenagers when he showed doubt about Mao's Cultural Revolution.

The alley girls make me feel like a foreigner. The place where I live is called the Institute, in a suburb of Beijing next to an ancient graveyard. The Institute is secured by high walls and patrolled by armed soldiers, bayoneted rifles on their shoulders and leather pistol holsters chained to their belts. Rumors are that the holsters are filled with old newspaper and the rifles are always empty, but the bayonets are real, sharp and shining. The heart of the Institute is a gray building secured by more soldiers. That is where my father as well as many fathers work, a research center for the Department of Nuclear Industry. Children like me growing up inside the Institute have different rules for life and games. We are not allowed to go out of the security gate of the Institute, not allowed to approach the gray building. The game we enjoy playing is to guess whose father is on "calculating duty"—our fathers go to another institute to use the *machine,* which we know nothing of until "computer" becomes a household word years later. Calculating duty is always performed at night, and every afternoon a father or two ride a luxury car into the dusk to a place nonexistent on any map. We watch the car drive by noiselessly, and then play the game. Every one of us pretends to be the child of the man behind the curtain. Only after asking questions and carefully examining one another's words do we find out who is telling the truth and who is making up stories.

That is where I am from, a world different from the world of the alley girls. I am surprised that they have never heard of the Institute or nuclear industry. In my world every child knows nuclear weapons, and we have made "atomic bomb" a nickname for the principal of our elementary school. But then I have to admit that they surely know other things that I do not know, like Truman and the Truman-eating tiger.

THE WIND STARTS at lunchtime, the wind from Siberia that brings winter to our city, whistling across the alley and shaking the tiles on the roof of every house. For the whole afternoon I kneel on a chair by the window, waiting for the wind to calm down so that I can go out to play with the alley girls. The blue sky has turned brownish gray, the sun behind the sand and dust pale like a dirty white plate. In the late afternoon, one by one the four boys of the Song family run into the yard, each of them sporting a newly shaved head. I run into the yard. "Hey," I shout in the wind, my eyes hurting from the dust. "What happened to your hair?"

"Gone," the youngest of the brothers shouts back. "Windy days are good for haircuts."

"Why?"

"No need to clean up. The wind does it," the third brother says, making a gesture of being blown away by the wind.

I laugh. I like the boys of the Song family, each one of

them knowing how to tell a joke and make people laugh. None of them is in school, the youngest one expelled from the high school for gang fights earlier in the year; nor is any of them working, since jobs are so scarce and the city is full of young idlers like the Song boys, *to-be-placed youths,* as they are called. The Song boys spend their days wandering in the city, picking fights with other boys and coming home with stories of their victory.

Mrs. Song sticks her head out their door and yells, "You money eaters! Who told you to shave your heads? I don't have money to buy you hats."

"Use the money we save on shampoo!" the oldest boy retorts.

I laugh and run back into the room.

"Out again to speak with the Song boys?" Mrs. Pang says, shoving coals into the burning belly of the stove.

"No," I lie, though I know Mrs. Pang will not be angry with me. Mrs. Pang was once a nanny for me, and she spoils me the way I imagined kindhearted women would spoil an orphan, loving me for whom I am, exactly the opposite of my mother, whose love I have to earn with great effort and with little success.

"They'll have a lot to worry about soon," Mrs. Pang sighs, placing a water kettle on the stove.

"Why?"

"They need to think about finding wives in a few years, right? If they do not have jobs and places to live, how can they get married?"

"Can they inherit their parents' jobs?"

"They sure can, but they only have two parents. What would the other two do?" Mrs. Pang says. "They learned nothing in school."

"I bet the oldest two will not inherit Mr. and Mrs. Song's jobs."

"How do you know?"

"I just know," I answer with a smile of secrecy. The oldest son of the Song family told me that their father worked in a factory making lightbulbs and their mother worked in a factory making light switches. "My mother clicks and my father is turned on. Perfect pair, huh?" he said, and was happy to see me laugh hard. Mr. Song is a quiet man, following every order of his loud wife, a loyal bulb always responding well to the light switch.

"Don't boast because you know too little," Mrs. Pang says. "Things change a lot. Within a blink a mountain flattens and a river dries up. Nobody knows who he'll become tomorrow."

NOT LONG BEFORE dinner, Mr. Pang comes back from work, chatting with Mr. Du in the yard about the weather before entering the room. Mr. Du rents the two small rooms on the eastern side of the quadrangle, and he pays the rent on time. He is a dutiful son, living with his old mother, who has been left paralyzed by a stroke. He does not have a wife, as nobody is willing to take care of his mother. Besides the Songs and the Dus, five other families live in the inner quadrangle, around a bigger yard that is connected to the front quadrangle with a moon-shaped door. The inner quadrangle used to be the Pangs' living quarters while the front quadrangle was for the servants. But of course that was before the *liberation*. Mr. and Mrs. Pang live now in the small quarters that once belonged to their chauffeur and his family, with a living room, a bedroom, and another bedroom that used to be shared by the Pangs' two daughters before they married, occupied by me when I visit. A small room next to the kitchen serves as Mr. Pang's study, the door always locked and the windows shut tight behind a heavy curtain.

"How was your day?" Mr. Pang comes in, putting his briefcase in the usual corner and hanging his coat and hat neatly behind the door.

"Good," I answer. "How was yours?"

"Working hard, as usual," Mr. Pang says and turns to Mrs. Pang. "How was your day?" It is the only thing he can think of saying to us at the end of the day. In the morning it is always, *How was your sleep?*

Mrs. Pang does not reply. Mr. Pang never earns a penny, hardworking as he is, six days a week and sometimes over-time on Sundays. Nobody knows what he does at work. He was kicked out of his working unit at the beginning of the Cultural Revolution, on the charge of being the son of a big landlord, an enemy of the proletarian class. After the Revo-lution, when he went back to his working unit in the Postal Department, he was told that his files had been lost and there was no record of his being employed there, even though every one of his colleagues had attended the meet-ing and voted for denouncing him as *a dog son of the evil landlord class*. Still he goes to work every day, taking the first of each month off to deliver copies of yet another letter to several sections in the Postal Department as well as the city government, appealing for an investigation of his history.

"A tiring day," Mr. Pang says, and sits down at the head of the table.

Mrs. Pang places a bowl of rice heavily in front of him. "Nobody pays you to work. What can you do? Just wasting your own life. Better if you could stay home and help me with the housework."

Mrs. Pang is the rice earner of the family. She was a nanny for years but I was the last kid she nannied. The year she spent with me made her age fast, as my mother always says when she blames me as the most difficult child in the world. After me, Mrs. Pang performs only small chores: buying groceries for some families in the alley, doing laundry for other families, and taking care of Mr. Du's paralyzed mother.

Mr. Pang does not reply and counts the grains of rice with his chopsticks.

"Please eat, Mr. Worker," Mrs. Pang says and exchanges a smile with me.

Mr. Pang eats silently. Dinner is the only time when Mr. Pang stays with us. Afterward, he goes directly to his study. One year he installed a folding bed in the study, and started to sleep there.

"What is he doing there in his study?" I ask when I am helping Mrs. Pang do the dishes.

"Heaven knows!"

"You know, he is the only one I know who has a study," I say. "I thought only rich people had studies and they never used them."

"That sounds like him."

"Why?"

"Because he does nothing in his study."

"But he is not rich."

"Well, he was at one time."

"Why does he still keep a study when he is no longer rich?"

"Because we still have these rooms left with us so he can play a rich man. Things could be worse—everything confiscated, not one penny left."

"Why? You are good people."

"Good people may not have good luck," Mrs. Pang says. "Remember the saying? *Bad luck always chooses a good man.*"

YET BAD LUCK has chosen Mr. Pang for another reason—he is a useless man.

"I wouldn't say his parents were parasites, but he sure is one," Mrs. Pang says. She likes to chat with me when she is hand-washing the laundry in the afternoon, a big washbasin in the middle of the living room, the winter sun pale on the floor.

"Yes, I think so, too." I dip my finger into the water to check the temperature. If Mrs. Pang does not forget to pour some hot water into the basin, I will be glad to catch the floating socks like slim fishes and wash them all, Mr. Pang's big gray socks last.

"How do you know?"

"I just know. He is a parasite and he lives off you."

Mrs. Pang laughs. "You sure know a lot. What else do you know?"

"He is very educated." I've learned that from the boys of the Song family. They said Mr. Pang was proof that school was useless.

"Ha, educated. You know how he got into the college? The entrance exam was very difficult, so he asked his younger brother to take it for him. His brother was very smart. That was how he got into college. If he took the test himself? Ugh, he would have to spend all his life taking the entrance exams."

"Really?"

"Yes. That's the story," Mrs. Pang says, handing a slice of soap to me.

"And then what?"

"Then? Then he went to the college and never took a single course for his engineering degree. He hired someone to take the courses and the tests for him for the diploma."

"But who would do that for him? Why get a diploma for someone else if he had taken all the tests?"

"There were always poor students willing to do that. They could not afford the tuition, but they did not have to pay a penny to receive a good education. The diploma? That was just a piece of paper. And that was all my husband got."

"Oh," I say, and throw Mr. Pang's sock back into the water, feeling cheated. "What was he doing in college?"

"Going to the theater. Practicing calligraphy and painting. Gardening. Teaching his parrots to recite poems. Thinking of himself as an artist. What else could he do? Just wasting his time and money."

This is the most incredible story I have ever heard, I think, unable to connect Mr. Pang, the gray-headed, hunchbacked man, with the young man squandering his money in the city. "How come you married him?" I ask.

"You know who I was then?" Mrs. Pang says. "My father was a landlord, too. We used to have servants, handmaids, nannies, chauffeurs, private teachers in our house. I was a parasite too."

From what I learned from books and movies, the daughters of landlords were always spoiled, ugly, and vicious. "You don't look like one," I say.

"I'm not anymore." Mrs. Pang smiles.

"But Mr. Pang still is."

"Yes, he still is."

"How come you married him?" I ask again.

"We got married because our parents wanted us to. That's my share of luck. No one will have more good luck or bad luck than heaven permits. And no one will have all good luck or all bad luck, like I once had a nanny and handmaids to do everything for me and now I am doing things for other people."

"But Mr. Pang always has good luck. He never works."

"That's his bad luck. He has nothing to do. He is useless."

THE NEXT SUMMER when I arrive at Mr. and Mrs. Pang's house, Mr. Pang has retired. Retired may be the wrong word because he has not been paid for years, nor is there any indication of a pension. According to the Song boys, who know every single story in the city, one Monday Mr. Pang found his desk assigned to another man and his stuff piled in the hallway, the handle of his favorite teacup missing. He insisted that he would not leave until they returned the handle of his teacup. "It's an old piece of China, older than your grandfather," he kept saying until people felt insulted by his comparison. They told him to shut up and go to the trash can along with his teacup.

That did it. Mr. Pang became a piece of trash. By the time I arrive that summer, he has locked himself up in his study along with the rooster Mrs. Pang has bought for my favorite dish. "Mr. Retired Worker!" Mrs. Pang knocks on the door when I arrive. "The kid is here."

Mr. Pang lifts a corner of the curtains up and looks at me with suspicion. I press my face on the window and peep in. There are shelves of ancient books in the room. His bed is unmade like a messed-up rooster nest. The rooster itself is sauntering and pecking around on his desk. White and gray rooster droppings are drying on the floor, perfectly round like large coins.

"Yuck," I say, pointing at the floor. Mr. Pang waves and tucks the curtain's corner into its place.

The fact that Mr. Pang is losing his mind makes me so unhappy that I do not go out to play with the alley girls. Even though I despise Mr. Pang as a parasite, I want him to be a healthy parasite. My knitted eyebrows make Mrs. Pang laugh at dinner. Mr. Pang is not coming to dinner with us anymore. He eats with the rooster in his room.

"What happened?" Mrs. Pang asks.

"Nothing," I say, shoveling the food into my mouth without swallowing.

"Mad at him?"

"Umm."

"Why?"

"I don't like him being this way."

"He lost his mind long ago. Don't worry about him."

I put down my chopsticks and walk around the table to Mrs. Pang. "I am mad at him for *you*." I hug Mrs. Pang and start to cry.

Mrs. Pang wipes my tears off with her hand, her palm scratching like sandpaper. "You are a very kind girl, even better than my own daughters," she says.

"Why?"

"They said they wished that they had never been born to us," Mrs. Pang says, still smiling. "You'll make them ashamed."

I go back to my seat and continue my dinner, not feeling better.

"Bad things happen," Mrs. Pang says.

"Not to you."

"Believe me, this is nothing. I have seen worse things."

"Why didn't you marry the younger brother?" I ask.

"Whose brother?"

"His brother, the one you said was very smart and took the entrance exam for him."

Mrs. Pang laughs as if she has heard the most absurd story in the world. I do not laugh with her. "He has been long gone. He died before he finished college," Mrs. Pang says.

"That's very sad."

"No, it's not that bad. Sometimes I feel glad for him to have died that early."

"Why?"

"Because he was a son of the landlord, too. He was such a bright and sensitive boy." Mrs. Pang looks across the table at the wall behind me for a moment and sighs. "He would have been killed by the Revolution."

"Why? Was he a bad guy?"

"You don't have to be a bad guy to get killed," Mrs. Pang says. "In '66 the Red Guards whipped to death eighty people from three families in the county next to my old home, and the youngest one was a three-year-old boy. I used to know some of them. Their grandfathers were landlords."

"Were they not bad guys?"

"They were people just like me," Mrs. Pang says. "That's why you would rather see someone you love die young than suffer from living."

I think for a moment. "My mom and dad never tell me these things."

"Maybe they will when you grow up."

"No, they won't. It is their occupational malady." In our

world in the Institute, a secret is a secret and it is always better to speak less than more.

AFTER DINNER EVERYONE in the quadrangle sits in the yard to enjoy the cooling air. Mr. Pang and Mr. Du's paralyzed mother are the only two people missing.

The jasmine bushes in the yard are blooming like crazy that summer, the fragrance so strong that one could become dizzy if sitting too close to the bushes. A horde of wasps has built a heavy hive under the roof, buzzing around the grapevines and tasting the grapes before they are large enough for an early harvest. The sticky juice from the pierced grapes is as corrosive as the most poisonous liquid. If you sit under the grape trellis long enough, you would think that you could see the grapes rotting one cluster after another, in a blink their smooth rinds replaced by ugly scars.

Mr. Du is the last one to sit down, after moving his orchids out of his room and carefully lining them under his window. Mr. Du is a big fan of orchids. What he raises are the most expensive species, the Gentleman's Orchid. That summer a small pot of blooming Gentleman's Orchid costs hundreds of yuan on the black market, more than the earnings of a worker for a year.

"Old Du, be careful of your orchids," Mr. Song says, waving his bamboo fan at a mosquito passing by. "Did you hear what happened last week in the Eastern Fourteen Alley? Someone broke into this old man's house and robbed him of all his orchids, and stabbed the old man, too."

Mr. Du nods without answering, his face squeezed into a smile that makes him look like a wrinkled baby. He is a janitor in a nearby warehouse. Apart from the bed in which his old mother moans and curses all day, all the other furniture in their rooms is made of the cardboard boxes he has taken home from the warehouse. Sheets of old calendars are pasted on the outside. One time I went with Mrs. Pang to their room and saw my favorite actress, Chen Chong, dangling from a cardboard cabinet. Underneath her smile were the printed words FIRST CLASS UREA, IMPORTED FROM JAPAN.

"What's the big fuss about the orchids?" Mrs. Song purses her lips. "I don't see anything special about them."

"What do you know, Ma?" the third son says. "It's said that they are Japanese orchids. Imported, understand? Just like Toshiba, Sony, Panasonic—Japanese products."

"Imported? No, no," the oldest son says. "The orchids are raised here, so they are at most *Japanese parts, Chinese assembled.*"

Everybody laughs. Japanese brands have become the symbol of modern life in Beijing. At lower prices, people can buy appliances of Japanese parts assembled in China, and still be able to boast about their second-class luxuries.

"Still, it is not worth losing one's life for the orchids," Mrs. Song says.

"*A bird is willing to die for a morsel of food. A man is willing to die for a penny of wealth,*" Mrs. Pang sighs. "They do not see the flowers. They see money."

"Not everyone." The second son points to Mr. Du. "Old Du here is an exception. Others raise the orchids for money. He is raising them as his wife and kids."

"Absolutely," the first son says to Mr. Du. "You know, you have every right to fight for your orchids. We won't blame you if you are killed by a robber. A man has to fight with someone who steals his wife and kids, right, Old Du?"

All of the Songs laugh. Mr. Du smiles again and does not say a word. His old mother is shouting indistinct words from inside her room. He nods again and moves the orchids back to his room, as tenderly as if they were his wife and children.

THAT NIGHT I can't sleep. Mosquitoes dash outside the netting around my head like small bombers. I lie on one side of the bed until the bamboo mat becomes sticky from my sweat, and roll to the other side, feeling the patterns left on my thighs by the woven bamboo. I am waiting for the burglar to break into our quadrangle, running away with the orchids as dear to Mr. Du as his own wife and children, leaving Mr. Du in a pool of blood. For the first time, I start to miss our apartment, secure within the high wall of the Institute.

The burglar does not come that night, nor the following nights. Still, the waiting keeps me awake night after night, until the dawn light sneaks in from above the curtain and the rooster's muffled song comes from Mr. Pang's tightly closed window. I stop going out to play with the alley girls, spending the hot afternoons taking long naps and waking up soaked in sweat. My head grows dizzy as I sit on the bed, looking out the window at the inner quadrangle, waiting for the Dimwit to come out of her room and dance in the yard. She is the only resident from the inner quadrangle who has ever crossed the moon-shaped door to the front quadrangle. The five families, reluctant to face Mrs. Pang in their everyday life, have built another door leading to the alley and blocked the moon-shaped door with barbed wire. The Dimwit once squeezed through the wire to talk to the Song boys, baring her breasts, which looked so stunningly huge that I was frightened speechless. When the Song boys targeted her breasts with slingshots, she giggled with them.

"What are you looking at?" Mrs. Pang comes in with a

cup of chrysanthemum tea. She always keeps the pot of tea cool in a basin of water while I nap.

"Where's Dimwit? I haven't seen her all week."

"She's not living here anymore. I must have forgotten to tell you. She was married off this last spring."

"Who would marry her?"

"Someone in her auntie's working unit. An older man. He married three times, and three times the wife died. They say he has the fate of a diamond."

"What does that mean?"

"Can you think of anything harder than diamond?"

"No."

"Right. His life is as hard as a diamond and whoever he marries will be damaged."

"Then why did they marry Dimwit to him?"

"Because she is a dimwit. A dimwit is empty, like air. Have you ever seen a diamond leave a scratch on the air?"

I think about Mrs. Pang's explanation. It makes sense and it does not make sense. I think about Mr. Pang. "What's Mr. Pang's fate, then? He is not a diamond, is he?"

"What do you think?" Mrs. Pang asks with a smile.

"Of course he is not," I say but my voice trails off. I know he has left scratches on Mrs. Pang's life. He has left scratches on my life, too.

"You are thinking too much these days," Mrs. Pang says, pinching my chin. "You are getting thinner. Your mom will wonder what has happened to you when she comes to pick you up. I'll make the chicken stew for you tomorrow."

"I NEED THE rooster tomorrow," Mrs. Pang says to Mr. Pang the second to the last evening. He is sneaking into the kitchen to get his dinner and a small handful of rice for the rooster. He smells horrible.

"Hear me?" Mrs. Pang raises her voice when he does not reply.

"Yes," Mr. Pang answers in a low voice, retreating toward the kitchen door. "Can I go buy a rooster for you?"

Mrs. Pang places the chopper on the chopping board with a bang. "I am going to make the chicken stew with *that* rooster in your room, and you go ahead and kill it after dinner," Mrs. Pang says, not looking back at Mr. Pang.

Mr. Pang does not reply, still keeping his head low. I walk around Mr. Pang and hug Mrs. Pang's back from behind with my sweaty arms. "Nana, I don't want to eat chicken stew."

"She doesn't want the chicken stew," Mr. Pang mumbles to Mrs. Pang's stiffened back.

Mrs. Pang does not return my hug and says with a strange flat voice, "I want the rooster for the chicken stew." I squeeze myself in between the counter and Mrs. Pang, looking up at her. Big drops of hot tears fall on my face.

Mr. Pang leaves for his room without making a sound, closing his door quietly as if fearing to let out the secret to the rooster. Mrs. Pang takes a towel and wipes my face clean. "Don't worry. He has to do it."

"Nana, let's not eat the chicken stew."

"We'll eat the chicken stew. We cannot let him live with the rooster forever."

THE YOUNGEST SON of the Song family is ambushed by a gang of boys from the West Forty Alley on his way to the grocery store for beer. When he comes back from the hospital, his stitched head is bound in thick blood-stained gauze.

Good that he has his head shaved like a shining lightbulb that summer, I am about to comment to him but decide not to. "Clean-shaven heads are easy for doctors to sew up," I say in a low voice to myself, making sure the boy does not hear me.

"My head is an iron head," the boy says. He is sitting under the grape trellis and spitting bloody phlegm into the jasmine bush. "Believe me—the brick, this thick," he gestures with two fingers, "was broken in half by my head."

Mr. Du nods with his sad smile. He is the only one responding to the boy. The three brothers are occupied: the oldest boy is grinding a long knife on a grindstone, the screeching noise making my skin tight with goose bumps; the second boy is waving a long metal chain in the air. "I see you sons of a bitch are tired of living," he shouts to the imaginary enemies outside the wall. "Be patient. We are coming for your heads."

"Cut it out!" Mrs. Song comes out of the room and slaps a wet towel onto the swollen eye of her youngest son. "Nobody is going out tonight, you hear me?"

"Ma, what are you talking about?" the third son comes out of the kitchen with two choppers in his hands and says. "Boys of the Song family are not soft persimmons for others to squeeze."

"You're asking for death," Mrs. Song yells, banging the gate of the quadrangle closed and sitting in front of the gate. "Nobody is going out of this gate tonight!"

"What are you afraid of, Ma?" the oldest son says. "*A tree cannot live without the bark. A man cannot live without a face.* They have spat in our faces. What would we be if we let this pass? Ma, let me tell you, everyone dies. Death? Death is not a bad joke if told the right way."

The four boys stomp their feet on the ground and roar. Mrs. Song curses, shouting at her husband, asking for help. Mr. Song stands on the doorsill of their room and looks at his boys without speaking. The light switch is not functioning this time—Mr. Song is refusing to be turned on like an obeying bulb.

"Are you dead? Stop your sons."

"Let them go. They do what they have to," Mr. Song says, strolling across the yard. "How are the orchids?" he asks Mr. Du.

"Not bad. Not bad," Mr. Du mumbles, pruning the orchids with a pair of tiny scissors and smiling back.

Mrs. Pang comes out of the room and pulls me back. "Don't mind other people's business," she says, knocking on Mr. Pang's door. "Time for the rooster."

A pot of water is kept boiling on the stove for a long time before Mr. Pang comes out of his room with the rooster, both wings held tight in his big hand. He walks without looking at the boisterous sons of the Song family. The rooster itself is cooing and looking around with curiosity.

Mrs. Pang points to the chopper on the counter without speaking. She tries to drag me out of the kitchen but I keep holding on to the doorknob, looking up at Mr. Pang. He glances at the chopper and pulls a chair to sit down, holding the rooster between his arms.

"If nobody buys, nobody will sell you. If nobody eats, nobody will kill you. Rooster, it is not that I want to kill you, but you were born to fill people's stomachs," Mr. Pang mumbles and strokes the dark green feathers on the rooster's head. Then he turns to Mrs. Pang. "Don't scare the kid," he says in a gentle voice.

Mrs. Pang drags me away and closes the kitchen door behind me. The rooster squeals for a moment and stops. For some time we wait outside the door, until Mr. Pang comes out with a bag of bloodstained feathers, green and brown, wrapped up in a plastic sack. "It's ready," he says in a low voice, nodding at Mrs. Pang without looking up at her. Sweat smears his face.

"Where are you going with that?" Mrs. Pang points to the bag in Mr. Pang's hand.

"They are not going to the trash can," Mr. Pang mumbles, walking toward the jasmine bush.

The chicken stew is for the last dinner of my visit that summer. Coming to pick me up, my mother is the only one who touches it during the meal. On the bus ride from the Pangs' house to the Institute, I listen silently to her berating. Her volume becomes higher until all the passengers are staring at me, and in their scolding eyes I see me, an inconsiderate and impolite child who did not even bother to touch the best dish her old nanny cooked for her, especially a chicken stew that her nanny usually could not afford to eat.

I have to admit twice to my mistake, once to my mother and then in a louder voice so that all the passengers can hear me, before my mother drops the topic and the passengers turn their eyes away from my burning face. I watch my sandals and hum my favorite song to myself: "Let me sing a song to the Communist Party. The Party is dearer than my own mother. My mother only gives me a body. It is the Party who gives me a soul."

A LOT OF things have changed by the next year I go to the Pangs' for the summer. My favorite actress, Chen Chong, has disappeared to the other side of the ocean, waiting tables in a California restaurant, bearing the same smile she once did in the calendars on our wall. In the evening news-paper, I read an article deriding her for being a second-class resident and living on tips given by American capitalists, with long emotional paragraphs, as if working for a living was such a shame that the author could not bear the pain even of writing about it. "Sour grapes," my mother sneers when she reads the article.

Gentleman's Orchids have gone out of fashion. The price drops so fast that they now are cheaper than weeds, Mrs. Song says. Many growers have lost fortunes. Mr. Du may be the only person welcoming the news. He stops wor-rying about his orchids when he is working on his shift. The orchids grow better than at any time before, blooming with big golden-colored flowers as if they too have stopped fear-ing along with Mr. Du.

Mr. and Mrs. Song have both retired early, leaving their positions to the first and second sons. Mr. Pang's jasmine bushes are cut down by the Song family, making space for a new room built as the wedding room for their first son. In another couple of years a wife and a baby will be added to the quadrangle, both of them sharing the new room with the oldest Song boy. The quadrangle becomes so packed that in the summer evening there is not a trace of breeze across the yard, and the wind from Siberia will never reach the inside of the quadrangle again.

Mr. Pang found a job earlier that summer, introduced by my father to a small scientific-education publishing house as a temporary employee. His duties include putting printed subscription ads into envelopes and sealing the envelopes with paste. My father conceals the parts of Mr. Pang's his-tory about rooming with a rooster and cheating in college for his diploma, and the publishing house finally agrees to hire him on the condition that he does not get a lunch coupon and overtime compensation. On the first day of his new job, Mr. Pang is said to have colored his white hair to a shining black and to have worn a brand-new woolen Mao jacket, which makes him look younger than his actual age of sixty-three. When he gets his first month's pay, he takes a two-hour bus ride and arrives at our Institute in the late morning on a Sunday. For thirty minutes he begs the guards to let him in, and tries to convince them that he is a good citizen who works honestly and earns his living, and that he does not have a working ID only because the publishing house does not issue IDs for temporary workers.

For years I will not be able to stop imagining the scene of Mr. Pang bowing to the guards, who threaten to have him arrested if he does not leave, two live roosters in his hands cooing along with him. The sight of Mr. Pang wandering around our high walls for an hour with two roosters seems heartbreakingly comic, although it is not I who find him but my father, on the way back from an extended calculating duty. "Your father saved me again," is the first sentence Mr. Pang says to me when he enters our apartment, holding the two roosters up like the biggest trophies of his life.

The scene will come back to me sixteen years later, but at the moment I just laugh when the roosters finally escape his grip, fluttering their wings around in our apartment. In a few minutes my father will catch them again, and in a few hours they will fill our stomachs and then be forgotten. Life goes at small baby steps when one is young, but then it picks up speed and flies. In four years, my favorite actress, Chen Chong, will finish her table-waiting career and start as Joan Chen in Hollywood, an actress and a director, her smile still pretty as I remember, though she will never again be the sixteen-year-old girl on our wall. In another seven years, Mrs. Pang will be leaving me forever. She will have been blind for a year before her death. The last time I visit her, she will be touching my face and feeling my tears beneath her fingertips, and both of us will be pretending that the tears are not there and we are enjoying the chicken stew I cook for her the way she has taught me. In five more years, I will be in America, sitting in my small and humid apartment in a Midwest town, reading my father's letter about Mr. Pang's death, knowing that for the last sixteen years of his life, he has never missed one day of work, sealing envelopes with patience.

As if the death of Mr. Pang is a story that would not hurt if only told by the Song boys, I imagine the four brothers talking about his death, out of boredom, out of the need to tell a joke. I have not seen the boys since the alley was torn down and the residents were moved out of the city to the suburban apartment complexes. I cannot imagine the lives of the boys and their families, the apartments gray and small as pigeon cages. What I see is the clean-shaven heads of the four boys, still in their twenties, talking and laughing and spitting and picking unripe grapes to shoot at one another.

"Wasn't Mr. Pang an old fool?" one brother would say. "Thirty-three yuan, just enough for a pack of beers? And to a teenager robber who used a fruit knife? The boy would not have one day of a better life with the money."

"The old man probably thought he earned the money himself," another brother would say. "He forgot that the robber had to work to earn the money, too. I bet the boy would have been pissed off with only thirty-three yuan in the wallet. Why not just let him have the money and be pissed off?"

"Like Mrs. Pang always said: A bird is willing to die for a

morsel of food; a man is willing to die for a penny of wealth," a brother would say. "When Mr. Pang's soul goes to the graveyard court to report his arrival, the judge would say: What? For thirty-three yuan you let yourself be stabbed? You were even stupider than me in my last life."

"What does that mean?"

"The judge would then say: You don't remember me? In my last life, I was that old man in East Fourteen Alley. Remember? I was stabbed by the robber of my Gentleman's Orchids!"

I imagine the Song boys laugh together, the way they used to laugh at all the people in the world. Death is not a bad joke if told the right way, yet I do not see a right way. I start to understand what Mrs. Pang said about death long ago, that one would rather see beloved ones die instead of suffering. It comforts me that she would not have to see Mr. Pang's death, and have to listen to the jokes told by the Song boys. It comforts me that not one more scratch would have to be left on her life, and I am the only one to live with the awkward joke that Mr. Pang's death makes.

But on second thought, I wish that Mrs. Pang had lived long enough. I wish we would sit together and fold his clothes for the last time. I wish Mrs. Pang would smile at me when she puts away Mr. Pang's clothes, and I would know that she is proud of him, earning his life between hills of envelopes at seventy-nine, being a useful man, defending himself, dying with dignity.

Persimmons

APRIL COMES AND APRIL GOES, AND MAY, AND June, all passing by without shedding a drop of rain. The sky has been a blue desert since spring. The sun rises every morning, a bright white disc growing larger and hotter each day. Cicadas drawl halfheartedly in the trees. The reservoir outside the village has shrunken into a bathtub for the boys, peeing at one another in the waist-deep water. Two girls, four or five, stand by the main road, their bare arms waving like desperate wings of baby birds as they chant to the motionless air, "Come the east wind. Come the west wind. Come the east-west-north-south wind and cool my armpits."

Now that July has only to move its hind foot out the door in a matter of days, we have started to wish, instead of rain, that no rain will fall and the drought will last till the end of the harvest season. Peasants as we are, and worrying about the grainless autumn as we are, the drought has, to our surprise, brought a languid satisfaction to our lives. Every day, from morning till evening, we sit under the old pagoda tree, smoking our pipes and moving our bodies only when the tree's shade threatens to leave us to the full spotlight of the sunshine. Our women are scratching their heads to come up with decent meals for us at home. The rice from last year will be running out soon, and before that, our women's hair will be thinning from too much scratching until they will all go bald, but this, like all the minor tragedies in the world, has stopped bothering us. We sit and smoke until our daily bags of tobacco leaves run out. We stuff grass roots and half-dead leaves into the bags, and when they run out, we smoke dust.

"Heaven's punishment, this drought." Someone, one of us, finally speaks after a long period of silent smoking.

"Yes, too many deaths."

"In that case, Heaven will never be happy again. People always die."

"And we'll never get a drop of rain."

"Suits me well. I'm tired of farming anyway."

"Yeah, right. Heaven comes to spank you, and you hurry up to bare your butts and say, Come and scratch me, I've got an itch here."

"It's called optimism, better than crying and begging for pardon."

"A soft persimmon is what you are. I would just grab His pants and spank Him back."

"Whoa, a hero we've got here."

"Why not?"

"Because we were born soft persimmons. See any hero coming out of a persimmon?"

"Lao Da."

"Lao Da? They popped his brain like a watermelon."

Lao Da was one of us. He should have been sitting here with us, smoking and waiting for his turn to speak out a line or two, to agree, or to contradict. When night falls, he

would, like all of us, walk home and dote on his son, dripping drops of rice wine from his chopsticks to the boy's
mouth. Lao Da would have never bragged about being a
hero, a man like him, who knew his place between the sky
and the earth. But the thing is, Lao Da was executed before
this drought began. On New Year's Eve, he went into the
county seat and shot seventeen people, fourteen men and
three women, in seventeen different houses, sixteen of them
dead on the spot, and the seventeenth lived only to see half
a day of the new year.

"If you were born a soft persimmon, you'd better stay
one"—someone says the comforting old wisdom.

"Persimmons are not born soft."

"But they are valued for their softness."

"Their ripeness."

"What then if we stay soft and ripened?"

"Heaven will squeeze us until He gets tired of squeez-
ing."

"He may even start to like us because we are so much
fun for Him."

"We'll just have our skins left by then."

"Better than having no skins."

"Better than having a bullet pop your brain."

"Better than having no son to inherit your name."

Silent for a moment, we all relish the fact that we are
alive, with boys to carry on our family names. Last year at
this time, Lao Da's son was one of the boys, five years old,
running behind older boys like all small kids do, picking up
the cicadas that the older boys shot down with their sling
guns, adding dry twigs and dead leaves to the fire that was lit
up to roast the bodies, waiting for his share of a burned ci-
cada or two.

"Lao Da's son died a bad one."

"As if there is a good way to die!"

"Those seventeen, weren't theirs good? Fast and painless."

"But in the city, they said those seventeen all died badly."

"Mercilessly murdered—wasn't that how they put it in the newspapers?"

"But that's true. They were murdered."

"True, but in the city, they wouldn't say the boy died badly. They didn't even mention Lao Da's son."

"Of course they wouldn't. Who would want to hear about a murderer's son? A dead son, not to mention."

"Even if they had written about him, what could they have said?"

"Drowned in a swimming accident, that's what was written in his death certificate."

"An accident happens every day, they would say."

"The boy's death wasn't worth a story."

The seventeen men and women's stories, however, were read aloud to us at Lao Da's trial, their enlarged pictures looking down at us from the top of the stage of a theater, a makeshift courthouse to contain the audience. We no longer remember their names, but some of the faces, a woman in heavy makeup who looked like a girl we were all obsessed with when we were young, a man with a sinister mole just below his left eye, another man with a pair of caterpillarlike eyebrows, these faces have stuck with us ever since. So have a few of the stories. A man who had been ice-swimming for twenty years and had never been ill for one day of his adult life. A mother of a teenage girl who had died earlier that year from leukemia. An official and his young secretary, who, as we heard from rumors, had been having an affair, but in the read-aloud stories, they were both the dear husband and wife to their spouses. The stories went on, and after a while we dozed off. What was the point of telling these dead people's stories to us? Lao Da had no chance of getting away. He turned himself in to the police, knowing he would get a death sentence. Why not spare those relatives the embarrassment of wailing in the court? Besides, no story was read aloud about Lao Da. He was an atrocious criminal was all that was said about him.

"Think about it: Lao Da was the only one who died a good death."

"A worthy one."

"Got enough companions for the trip to the next world."

"Got us into trouble, too."

"It wasn't his mistake. Heaven would've found another reason to squeeze us."

"True. Lao Da was just an excuse."

"Maybe—I have been thinking—maybe Heaven is angry not because of Lao Da, but for him?"

"How?"

"I heard from my grandpa, who heard from his grandpa, that there was this woman who was beheaded as a murderer, and for three years after her execution, not a drop of rain fell on the area."

"I heard that from my grandpa, too. Heaven was avenging the woman."

"But she was wronged. She did not kill her husband."

"True."

Lao Da was not wronged. You killed seventeen people and you had to pay with your life. Even Lao Da nodded in agreement when the judge read the sentence. He bowed to the judge and then to the guards when he was escorted off the stage. "I'm leaving one step earlier," he said. "Will be waiting for you on the other side." The guards, the judge, and the officials on and off the stage, they all tried to turn their eyes away from Lao Da, but he was persistent in his farewell. "Come over soon. Don't let me wait for too long," he said. We never expected Lao Da to have such a sense of humor. We grinned at him and he grinned back, but for a short moment only, as the judge waved for two more guards to push him to the backstage before he had time to give out too many invitations.

"Lao Da was a man."

"Spanked Heaven."

"But who's got the upper hand now?"

"It means nothing to Lao Da now. He had his moment."

"But it matters to us. We are punished for those who were wronged by death."

"Who?"

"Those seventeen."

"Not the wife of the cuckold, I hope."

"Certainly not. She deserved it."

"That woman was smaller than a toenail of Lao Da's wife."

"That woman was cheaper than a fart of Lao Da's wife."

"True."

"Good woman Lao Da had as a wife."

"Worthy of his life."

We nod, and all think about Lao Da's wife, secretly comparing her with our own women. Lao Da's wife worked like a man in the field and behaved like a woman at home. She was plump, and healthy, and never made a sound when Lao Da beat her for good or bad reasons, or for no reason at all. Our wives are not as perfect. If they are not too thin they are too fat. If they are diligent, they do not leave us alone, nagging us for our laziness. They scream when beaten; even worse, sometimes they fight back.

"That good woman deserved better luck."

"She deserved another son."

"But her tubes were tied."

"The poor woman would've lived if not for the Birth Control Office."

"A group of pests they are, aren't they?"

The Birth Control Office had been after Lao Da and his wife when they had not reported to the office after their first-born. *One child per family,* they brushed in big red words on Lao Da's house. *Only pigs and dogs give birth to more than one child,* they wrote. But Lao Da and his woman never gave up. They played hide-and-seek with the Birth Control Office, hiding in different relatives' places when the woman's belly was growing big. After three daughters and a big debt for the fines, they finally had a son. The day the boy turned a hundred days old, Lao Da killed a goat and two suckling pigs for a banquet; afterward, the wife was sent to the clinic to have her tubes triumphantly tied.

"What's the point of living if she could not bear another son for Lao Da? What's the use of a hen if it doesn't lay eggs?"

"True."

"But that woman, she was something."

"Wasn't she?"

We exchange looks of awe, all knowing that our own women would never have had the courage to do what Lao Da's wife did. Our women would have screamed and begged when we faced no other choices but divorcing them for a fertile belly, but Lao Da's wife, she never acted like an ordinary woman. When we, along with Lao Da, dived into the reservoir to look for the body of Lao Da's son, she drank all the pesticide she could lay her hands on, six bottles in a row, and lay down in bed. Six bottles of pesticide with that strength could cut her into pieces, but she did not make a single sound, her jaws clenched, waiting for death.

"An extraordinary woman."

"Maybe Heaven is angry on her behalf."

"She was not wronged by anybody."

"But her soul was let down."

"By whom?"

"Lao Da."

"Lao Da avenged her, and their son."

"Was it what she wanted?"

"What did she want?"

"Listen, she was making room for a new wife, so Lao Da could have more sons. She didn't poison herself just to make Lao Da lose his mind and carry out some stupid plan to shoot seventeen people. Think about it. Lao Da got everything wrong."

"Her death could have borne more fruits."

"That's true. Now she died for nothing."

"And Lao Da, too."

"And those seventeen."

"And the three daughters, orphaned for nothing."

We shake our heads, thinking about the three girls, their screaming and crying piercing our eardrums when the county officials grabbed their arms and pushed them into the jeep. They were sent to different orphanages in three counties, bad seeds of a cold-blooded killer. Lao Da should have listened to us and drowned them right after they were born, sparing them their troubles of living in pain.

"Lao Da could have done better."

"Reckless man."

We could have made a wiser choice than Lao Da. We would have let the dead be buried and gone on living, finding a new wife to bear a new son, working, our backs bent, to feed the wife and the children. There would be the pain, naturally, of waking up to the humiliation of being a soft persimmon, but humiliation does not kill a man. Nothing beats clinging to this life. Death ferries us nowhere.

"One man's mistake can capsize a whole ship of people."

"True."

"Death of a son is far from the biggest tragedy."

"Death of anybody shouldn't be an excuse to lose one's mind."

"But Lao Da had the right to seek justice for his boy."

"Justice? What kind of justice is there for us?"

"If one kills, one has to pay with his life. Nothing's wrong with the old rule. The man who killed Lao Da's son should have been punished."

"He was punished all right. The first one Lao Da shot that night, wasn't he?"

"Two shots in the brain. Two shots in the heart."

"In front of his woman."

"Well done it was."

"Couldn't be better."

"When I heard the news, I felt I had just downed a full pot of sorghum wine."

"It beats the best wine out there."

"See, that's what justice is."

"True. One can never run away from justice's palm."

"You just have to wait for the time."

"Heaven sees, doesn't He?"

"But if He does see, why are we punished? What kind of justice is this?"

"I've told you: there is no justice for us persimmons."

"If you kill one person, you are a murderer. If you kill a lot, you are a hero."

"Lao Da killed seventeen."

"Not quite enough."

"If you've made a point, you are a hero. If you've failed to make a point, you are nothing."

"What's the point to make?"

"There should be an order for everyone to follow."

"A dreamer is what you are, asking for the impossible."

"We all asked for that at the riot, but it didn't get us anywhere."

"That was because we gave up."

"Bullshit. What's the point fighting for a dead boy?"

"True."

"What's the point risking our lives for a nonexistent order?"

"True."

We all nod, eager to shoo away the tiny doubt that circles us like a persistent fly. Of course, we did what we could—after the boy was found in the water, we marched together with his little body to the county seat, asking for justice. Hoes and spades and axes and our fists and throats we all brought with us, but when the government sent the troop of armed police in our direction, we decided to go back home. Violence will not solve your problem, we said to Lao Da. Go to the court and sue the man; follow what the law says, we told Lao Da.

"Maybe we shouldn't have put the seed in Lao Da's mind to sue the man."

"Had I been him, I would have done the same."

"The same what? Going around the city and asking justice for his son's death? His son was drowned in a swimming accident—black words on a white page in his death certificate."

"The other boys told a different story."

"Why would the court want to listen to the story?"

We sit and smoke and wait for someone to answer the question. A group of boys are returning to the village from the reservoir, all dripping wet. Lao Da's boy would never have been drowned if there had been a drought last year. We don't worry about our sons this year, even the youngest ones, who cannot swim well. But last year was a different story. Last year's reservoir was deep enough to kill Lao Da's son.

"But don't you think the officials made some mistakes too? What if they gave Lao Da some money to shut him up?"

"What if they put that man in jail, even for a month or two?"

"Isn't that a smart idea? Or pretend to put the man in jail?"

"Yes, just tell Lao Da the man got his punishment."

"At least treat Lao Da a little better."

"Would have saved themselves."

"But how could they have known? They thought Lao Da was a soft persimmon."

"Squeezed him enough for fun."

"Squeezed a murderer out of it."

"Lao Da was the last one you would think to snap like that."

"Amazing how much one could take and then all of a sudden he broke."

"True."

"But back to my point, what's the good losing one's mind over a dead son and a dead wife?"

"Easier said than done."

"True. How many times did we tell him to stop pursuing the case?"

"Sometimes a man sets his mind on an idea, and he becomes a hunting dog, only seeing one thing."

"And now we are punished for his stupidity."

We shake our heads, sorry for Lao Da, more so for ourselves. Lao Da should have listened to us. Instead, he was writing down the names and addresses of those officials who had treated him like a dog. How long he had been preparing for the killing we do not know. He had the patience to wait for half a year until New Year's Eve, the best time to carry out a massive murder, when all the people were staying home for the year-end banquet.

"At least we have to give Lao Da the credit for carrying out his plan thoroughly."

"He had a brain when it came to revenge."

"And those seventeen dead souls. Think about how shocked they were when they saw Lao Da that night."

"I hope they had time to regret what they had done to Lao Da."

"I hope their families begged Lao Da for them as Lao Da had begged them for his boy."

"You'd never know what could come from a soft persimmon."

"I hope they were taught a lesson."

"They're dead."

"Then someone else was taught the lesson."

"Quiet! Be careful in case someone from the county hears you."

"So hot they won't be here."

"The reservoir is not deep enough for them now."

"The reservoir is really the cause of all these bad things. Think about the labors we put into the reservoir."

We nod and sigh. A few years ago, we put all our free time into building the reservoir, hoping to end our days of relying on Heaven's mood for the rain. The reservoir soon became an entertaining site for the county officials. On summer afternoons, they came in jeeps, swimming in our water, fishing our fish. The man was one of the judges—but what indeed was his line of work we never got to know, as we call everybody working in the county court "judge." That judge and his companions came, all drunk before they went into the water. Something Lao Da's son said, a joke maybe, or just a nickname he gave to the judge, made him angry. He picked up Lao Da's son and threw him into the deeper water of the reservoir. A big splash the other boys remembered. They cried, begged, but the judges all said it would teach the little bastard a lesson. The boys sent the fastest one among them to run for help. Lao Da's son was found later that night, his eyelids, lips, fingers, toes, and penis all eaten into bad shapes by the feasting fish.

"Remember, Lao Da was one of those who really pushed for the reservoir."

"He worked his back bent for it."

"The poor man didn't know what he was sweating for."

"None of us knows."

"At least we don't have to sweat this summer."

"Of course, you don't sweat waiting for death."

"Death? No, not that bad."

"Not that bad? Let me ask you—what will we feed our women and kids in the winter?"

"Whatever is left from the autumn."

"Nothing will be left."

"Then feed them our cows and horses."

"Then what?"

"Then we'll all go to the county and become beggars."

"It's illegal to beg."

"I don't care."

"If you want to do something illegal, why be a beggar and be spat at by everybody? I would go to the county and request to be fed."

"How?"

"With my fist and my axe."

"Don't talk big. We were there once with our fists and our axes."

"But that was for the dead boy. This time it'll be for our own sons."

"Do you think it'll work?"

"You have to try."

"Nonsense. If it works, it would have worked last time. Lao Da wouldn't have had to kill and we wouldn't have to be punished."

Nobody talks. The sun has slowly hauled itself to the southwest sky. The cicadas stop their chanting, but before we have time to enjoy the silence, they pick up the old tune again. Some of us draw and puff imaginary smokes from our pipes that are no longer lit; others pick up dry twigs from the ground, sketching in the dust fat clouds, heavy with rain.

A Thousand Years
of Good Prayers

A ROCKET SCIENTIST, MR. SHI TELLS PEOPLE when they ask about his profession in China. Retired, he then adds, out of modesty, when people marvel. Mr. Shi learned the phrase from a woman during a layover at Detroit, when he tried to explain to her his work, drawing pictures when his English failed to help. "A rocket scientist!" the woman exclaimed, laughing out loud.

People he meets in America, already friendly, seem more so when they learn his profession, so he likes to repeat the words whenever possible. Five days into his visit at his daughter's place, in this Midwest town, Mr. Shi has made quite a few acquaintances. Mothers with babies in strollers wave at him. An old couple, the husband in suit and the wife in skirt, show up in the park every morning at nine o'clock, her hand on his arm; they stop and greet him, the husband always the one speaking, the wife smiling. A woman living in the retirement home a block away comes to talk to him. She is seventy-seven, two years his senior, and was originally from Iran. Despite the fact they both speak little English, they have no problem understanding each other, and in no time they become friends.

"America good country," she says often. "Sons make rich money."

America is indeed a good country. Mr. Shi's daughter works as a librarian in the East Asian department in the college library and earns more in a year than he made in twenty.

"My daughter, she make lots of money, too."

"I love America. Good country for everybody."

"Yes, yes. A rocket scientist I am in China. But very poor. Rocket scientist, you know?" Mr. Shi says, his hands making a peak.

"I love China. China a good country, very old," the woman says.

"America is young country, like young people."

"America a happy country."

"Young people are more happy than old people," Mr. Shi says, and then realizes that it is too abrupt a conclusion. He himself feels happier at this moment than he remembers he ever did in his life. The woman in front of him, who loves everything with or without a good reason, seems happy, too.

Sometimes they run out of English. She switches to Persian, mixed with a few English words. Mr. Shi finds it hard to speak Chinese to her. It is she who carries the conversation alone then, for ten or twenty minutes. He nods and smiles effusively. He does not understand much of what she is saying, but he feels her joy in talking to him, the same joy he feels listening to her.

Mr. Shi starts to look forward to the mornings when he sits in the park and waits for her. "Madam" is what he uses to address her, as he has never asked her name. Madam wears colors that he does not imagine a woman of her age, or where she came from, would wear, red and orange and purple and yellow. She has a pair of metal barrettes, a white elephant and a blue-and-green peacock. They clasp on her thin hair in a wobbly way that reminds him of his daughter when she was a small child—before her hair was fully grown, with a plastic butterfly hanging loose on her forehead. Mr. Shi, for a brief moment, wants to tell Madam how much he misses the days when his daughter was small and life was hopeful. But he is sure, even before he starts, that his English would fail him. Besides, it is never his habit to talk about the past.

IN THE EVENINGS, when his daughter comes home, Mr. Shi has the supper ready. He took a cooking class after his wife died, a few years ago, and ever since has studied the culinary art with the same fervor with which he studied mathematics and physics when he was a college student. "Every man is born with more talents than he knows how to use," he says at dinner. "I would've never imagined taking up cooking, but here I am, better than I imagined."

"Yes, very impressive," his daughter says.

"And likewise"—Mr. Shi takes a quick glance at his daughter—"life provides more happiness than we ever know. We have to train ourselves to look for it."

His daughter does not reply. Despite the pride he takes in his cooking and her praises for it, she eats little and eats out of duty. It worries him that she is not putting enough enthusiasm into life as she should be. Of course, she has her reasons, newly divorced after seven years of marriage. His ex-son-in-law went back to Beijing permanently after the divorce. Mr. Shi does not know what led the boat of their marriage to run into a hidden rock, but whatever the reason is, it must not be her fault. She is made for a good wife, soft-voiced and kindhearted, dutiful and beautiful, a younger version of her mother. When his daughter called to inform him of the divorce, Mr. Shi imagined her in inconsolable pain, and asked to come to America, to help her recover. She refused, and he started calling daily and pleading, spending a good solid month of his pension on the long-distance bill. She finally agreed when he announced that his wish for his seventy-fifth birthday was to take a look at America. A lie it was, but the lie turned out to be a good reason. America is worth taking a look at; more than that, America makes him a new person, a rocket scientist, a good conversationalist, a loving father, a happy man.

After dinner, Mr. Shi's daughter either retreats to her bedroom to read or drives away and comes home at late hours. Mr. Shi asks to go out with her, to accompany her to the movies he imagines that she watches alone, but she refuses in a polite but firm manner. It is certainly not healthy for a woman, especially a contemplative woman like his daughter, to spend too much time alone. He starts to talk more to tackle her solitude, asking questions about the part of her life he is not witnessing. How was her work of the day? he asks. Fine, she says tiredly. Not discouraged, he asks about her colleagues, whether there are more females than males, how old they are, and, if they are married, whether they have children. He asks what she eats for lunch and whether she eats alone, what kind of computer she uses, and what books she reads. He asks about her old school friends, people he believes she is out of contact with because of the shame of the divorce. He asks about her plan for the future, hoping she understands the urgency of her situation. Women in their marriageable twenties and early thirties are like lychees that have been picked from the tree; each passing day makes them less fresh and less desirable, and only too soon will they lose their value, and have to be gotten rid of at a sale price.

Mr. Shi knows enough not to mention the sale price. Still, he cannot help but lecture on the fruitfulness of life. The more he talks, the more he is moved by his own patience. His daughter, however, does not improve. She eats less and becomes quieter each day. When he finally points out that she is not enjoying her life as she should, she says, "How do you get this conclusion? I'm enjoying my life all right."

"But that's a lie. A happy person will never be so quiet!"

She looks up from the bowl of rice. "Baba, you used to be very quiet, remember? Were you unhappy then?"

Mr. Shi, not prepared for such directness from his daughter, is unable to reply. He waits for her to apologize and change the topic, as people with good manners do when they realize they are embarrassing others with their questions, but she does not let him go. Her eyes behind her glasses, wide open and unrelenting, remind him of her in her younger years. When she was four or five, she went after him every possible moment, asking questions and demanding answers. The eyes remind him of her mother too; at one time in their marriage, she gazed at him with this questioning look, waiting for an answer he did not have for her.

He sighs. "Of course I've always been happy."

"There you go, Baba. We can be quiet *and* happy, can't we?"

"Why not talk about your happiness with me?" Mr. Shi says. "Tell me more about your work."

"You didn't talk much about your work either, remember? Even when I asked."

"A rocket scientist, you know how it was. My work was confidential."

"You didn't talk much about anything," his daughter says.

Mr. Shi opens his mouth but finds no words coming. After a long moment, he says, "I talk more now. I'm improving, no?"

"Sure," his daughter says.

"That's what you need to do. Talk more," Mr. Shi says. "And start now."

His daughter, however, is less enthusiastic. She finishes her meal quickly in her usual silence and leaves the apartment before he finishes his.

THE NEXT MORNING, Mr. Shi confesses to Madam, "The daughter, she's not happy."

"Daughter a happy thing to have," Madam says.

"She's divorced."

Madam nods, and starts to talk in Persian. Mr. Shi is not sure if Madam knows what divorce means. A woman so boldly in love with the world like her must have been shielded from life's unpleasantness, by her husband, or her sons maybe. Mr. Shi looks at Madam, her face brightened by her talking and laughing, and almost envies her for the energy that his daughter, forty years younger, does not possess. For the day Madam wears a bright orange blouse with prints of purple monkeys, all tumbling and grinning; on her head she wears a scarf with the same pattern. A displaced woman she is, but no doubt happily displaced. Mr. Shi tries to recall what he knows about Iran and the country's recent history; with his limited knowledge, all he can conclude is that Madam must be a lucky woman. A lucky man he is, too, despite all the big and small imperfections. How extraordinary, Mr. Shi thinks, that Madam and he, from different worlds and with different languages, have this opportunity to sit and talk in the autumn sunshine.

"In China we say, *Xiu bai shi ke tong zhou*," Mr. Shi says when Madam stops. It takes three hundred years of prayers to have the chance to cross a river with someone in the same boat, he thinks of explaining to Madam in English, but then, what's the difference between the languages? Madam would understand him, with or without the translation. *"That we get to meet and talk to each other—it must have taken a long time of good prayers to get us here,"* he says in Chinese to Madam.

Madam smiles in agreement.

"There's a reason for every relationship, that's what the saying means. Husband and wife, parents and children, friends and enemies, strangers you bump into in the street. It takes three thousand years of prayers to place your head side by side with your loved one's on the pillow. For father and daughter? A thousand years, maybe. People don't end up randomly as father and daughter, that's for sure. But the daughter, she doesn't understand this. She must be thinking I'm a nuisance. She prefers I shut up because that's how she's known me always. She doesn't understand that I didn't talk much with her mother and her because I was a rocket scientist back then. Everything was confidential. We worked all day and when evening came, the security guards came to collect all our notebooks and scratch papers. We signed our names on the archive folders, and that was a day's work. Never allowed to tell our family what we were doing. We were trained not to talk."

Madam listens, both hands folding on her heart. Mr. Shi hasn't been sitting so close to a woman his age since his wife died; even when she was alive, he had never talked this much to her. His eyes feel heavy. Imagine he's traveled half a world to his daughter, to make up for all the talks he denied her when she was younger, but only to find her uninterested in his words. Imagine Madam, a stranger who does not even know his language, listens to him with more understanding. Mr. Shi massages his eyes with his two thumbs. A man his age shouldn't indulge himself in unhealthy emotions; he takes long breaths, and laughs slightly. *"Of course, there's a reason for a bad relationship, too—I must be praying halfheartedly for a thousand years for the daughter."*

Madam nods solemnly. She understands him, he knows, but he does not want to burden her with his petty unhappiness. He rubs his hands as if to get rid of the dust of memory. "Old stories," he says in his best English. "Old stories are not exciting."

"I love stories," Madam says, and starts to talk. Mr. Shi listens, and she smiles all the time. He looks at the grinning monkeys on her head, bobbing up and down when she breaks out laughing.

"Lucky people we are," he says after she finishes talking. "In America, we can talk anything."

"America good country." Madam nods. "I love America."

THAT EVENING, Mr. Shi says to his daughter, "I met this Iranian lady in the park. Have you met her?"

"No."

"You should meet her sometime. She's so very optimistic. You may find her illuminating for your situation."

"What's my situation?" his daughter asks without looking up from her food.

"You tell me," Mr. Shi says. When his daughter makes no

move to help the conversation, he says, "You're experiencing a dark time."

"How do you know she would shed light on my life?"

Mr. Shi opens his mouth, but cannot find an answer. He is afraid that if he explains he and Madam talk in different languages, his daughter will think of him as a crazy old man. Things that make sense at one time suddenly seem absurd in a different light. He feels disappointed in his daughter, someone he shares a language with but with whom he can no longer share a dear moment. After a long pause, he says, "You know, a woman shouldn't ask such direct questions. A good woman is deferential and knows how to make people talk."

"I'm divorced, so certainly I'm not a good woman according to your standard."

Mr. Shi, thinking his daughter is unfairly sarcastic, ignores her. "Your mother was an example of a good woman."

"Did she succeed in making you talk?" his daughter asks, and her eyes, looking directly into his, are fiercer than he knows.

"Your mother wouldn't be so confrontational."

"Baba, first you accused me of being too quiet. I start to talk, and you are saying I'm talking in a wrong way."

"Talking is not only asking questions. Talking is you telling people how you feel about them, and inviting them to tell you how they feel about you."

"Baba, since when did you become a therapist?"

"I'm here to help you, and I'm trying my best," Mr. Shi says. "I need to know why you ended up in a divorce. I need to know what went wrong and help you to find the right person the next time. You're my daughter and I want you to be happy. I don't want you to fall twice."

"Baba, I didn't ask you before, but how long do you plan to stay in America?" his daughter says.

"Until you recover."

His daughter stands up, the legs of the chair scraping the floor.

"We're the only family for each other now," Mr. Shi says, almost pleading, but his daughter closes her bedroom door before he says more. Mr. Shi looks at the dishes that are barely touched by his daughter, the fried tofu cubes stuffed with chopped mushrooms, shrimps, and ginger, the collage of bamboo shoots, red peppers, and snow peas. Even though his daughter admires his cooking every evening, he senses the halfheartedness in her praise; she does not know the cooking has become his praying, and she leaves the prayers unanswered.

"THE WIFE WOULD'VE done a better job of cheering the daughter up," Mr. Shi says to Madam the next morning. He feels more at ease speaking to her in Chinese now. "They were closer to each other. Wasn't that I was not close to them. I loved them dearly. It's what happened when you were a rocket scientist. I worked hard during the day, and at night I couldn't stop thinking about my work. Everything was confidential so I couldn't talk to my family about what I was thinking about. But the wife, she was the most understanding woman in the world. She knew I was so occupied with my work, and she wouldn't interrupt my thoughts, and wouldn't let the daughter, either. I know now that it was not healthy for the daughter. I should've left my working self in the office. I was too young to understand that. Now the daughter, she doesn't have anything to say to me."

Truly it was his mistake, never establishing a habit of

peak expectations?

talking to his daughter. But then, he argues for himself—in his time, a man like him, among the few chosen to work for a grand cause, he had to bear more duties toward his work than his family. Honorable and sad, but honorable more than sad.

At the dinner table that evening, Mr. Shi's daughter informs him that she's found a Chinese-speaking travel agency that runs tours both on the East Coast and the West. "You're here to take a look at America. I think it's best you take a couple of tours before winter comes."

"Are they expensive?"

"I'll pay, Baba. It's what you wanted for your birthday, no?"

She is his daughter after all; she remembers his wish and she honors it. But what she does not understand is that the America he wants to see is the country where she is happily married. He scoops vegetables and fish into her bowl. "You should eat more," he says in a gentle voice.

"So, I'm going to call them tomorrow and book the tours," his daughter says.

"You know, staying here probably does more good for me. I'm an old man now, not very good for traveling."

"But there's not much to see here."

"Why not? This is the America I wanted to see. Don't worry. I have my friends here. I won't be too much of an annoyance to you."

The phone rings before his daughter replies. She picks up the phone and automatically goes into her bedroom. He waits for the bang of the door. She never takes a call in front of him, even with strangers trying to sell her something on the phone. A few evenings when she talked longer and talked in a hushed voice, he had to struggle not to put his *beginning of communication?*

ear on the door and listen. This evening, however, she seems to have a second thought, and leaves the bedroom door open.

He listens to her speak English on the phone, her voice shriller than he has ever known it to be. She speaks fast and laughs often. He does not understand her words, but even more, he does not understand her manner. Her voice, too sharp, too loud, too immodest, is so unpleasant to his ears that for a moment he feels as if he had accidentally caught a glimpse of her naked body, a total stranger, not the daughter he knows.

He stares at her when she comes out of the room. She puts the receiver back, and sits down at the table without saying anything. He watches her face for a moment, and asks, "Who was it on the phone?"

"A friend."

"A male friend, or a female?"

"A male."

He waits for her to give further explanation, but she seems to have no such intention. After a while, he says, "Is this man—is he a special friend?"

"Special? Sure."

"How special is he?"

"Baba, maybe this'll make you worry less about me—yes, he is a very special one. More than a friend," his daughter says. "A lover. Do you feel better now that you know my life isn't as miserable as you thought?"

"Is he American?"

"An American now, yes, but he came from Romania."

At least the man grew up in a communist country, Mr. Shi thinks, trying to be positive. "Do you know him well? Does he understand you—where you were from, and your culture—well? Remember, you can't make the same mistakes twice. You have to be really careful."

"We've known each other for a long time."

"A long time? A month is not a long time!"

"Longer than that, Baba."

"One and half months at most, right? Listen, I know you are in pain, but a woman shouldn't rush, especially in your situation. Abandoned women—they make mistakes in loneliness!"

His daughter looks up. "Baba, my marriage wasn't what you thought. I wasn't abandoned." hm?

Mr. Shi looks at his daughter, her eyes candid with resolve and relief. For a moment he almost wants her to spare him any further detail, but like all people, once she starts talking, he cannot stop her. "Baba, we were divorced because of this man. I was the abandoner, if you want to use the term." oh snap.

"But why?"

"Things go wrong in a marriage, Baba."

"*One night of being husband and wife in bed makes them in love for a hundred days.* You were married for seven years! How could you do this to your husband? What was the problem, anyway, besides your little extramarital affair?" Mr. Shi says. A disloyal woman is the last thing he raised his daughter to be.

"There's no point talking about it now."

"I'm your father. I have a right to know," Mr. Shi says, banging on the table with a hand.

"Our problem was I never talked enough for my husband. He always suspected that I was hiding something from him because I was quiet." you were lol.

"You were hiding a lover from him."

Mr. Shi's daughter ignores his words. "The more he asked me to talk, the more I wanted to be quiet and alone. I'm not good at talking, as you've pointed out."

"But that's a lie. You just talked over the phone with such immodesty! You talked, you laughed, like a prostitute!"

Mr. Shi's daughter, startled by the vehemence of his words, looks at him for a long moment before she replies in a softer voice. "It's different, Baba. We talk in English, and it's easier. I don't talk well in Chinese."

"That's a ridiculous excuse!"

"Baba, if you grew up in a language that you never used to express your feelings, it would be easier to take up another language and talk more in the new language. It makes you a new person."

"Are you blaming your mother and me for your adultery?"

"That's not what I'm saying, Baba!"

"But isn't it what you meant? We didn't do a good job bringing you up in Chinese so you decided to find a new language and a new lover when you couldn't talk to your husband honestly about your marriage."

"You never talked, and Mama never talked, when you both knew there was a problem in your marriage. I learned not to talk."

"Your mother and I never had a problem. We were just quiet people."

"But it's a lie!"

"No, it's not. I know I made the mistake of being too preoccupied with my work, but you have to understand I was quiet because of my profession."

"Baba," Mr. Shi's daughter said, pity in her eyes. "You know it's a lie, too. You were never a rocket scientist. Mama knew. I knew. Everybody knew."

Mr. Shi stares at his daughter for a long time. "I don't understand what you mean."

"But you know, Baba. You never talked about what you did at work, true, but other people—they talked about you."

Mr. Shi tries to find some words to defend himself, but his lips quiver without making a sound.

His daughter says, "I'm sorry, Baba. I didn't mean to hurt you."

Mr. Shi takes long breaths and tries to maintain his dignity. It is not hard to do so, after all, as he has, for all his life, remained calm about disasters. "You didn't hurt me. Like you said, you were only talking about truth," he says, and stands up. Before he retreats to the guest bedroom, she says quietly behind him, "Baba, I'll book the tours for you tomorrow."

MR. SHI SITS in the park and waits to say his farewell to Madam. He has asked his daughter to arrange for him to leave from San Francisco after his tour of America. There'll still be a week before he leaves, but he has only the courage to talk to Madam one last time, to clarify all the lies he has told about himself. He was not a rocket scientist. He had had the training, and had been one for three years out of the thirty-eight years he worked for the Institute. *Hard for a young man to remain quiet about his work,* Mr. Shi rehearses in his mind. *A young rocket scientist, such pride and glory. You just wanted to share the excitement with someone.*

That someone—twenty-five years old, forty-two years ago—was the girl working on the card-punching machine for Mr. Shi. Punchers they were called back then, a profession that has long been replaced by more advanced computers, but of all the things that have disappeared from his life, a card puncher is what he misses most. *His* card puncher. "*Name is Yilan,*" Mr. Shi says aloud to the air, and someone greets the name with a happy hello. Madam is walking toward him with basket of autumn leaves. She picks up one and hands it to Mr. Shi. "Beautiful," she says.

Mr. Shi studies the leaf, its veins to the tiniest branches, the different shades of yellow and orange. Never before has he seen the world in such detail. He tries to remember the softened edges and dulled colors he was more used to, but like a patient with his cataracts taken away, he finds everything sharp and bright, appalling yet attractive. "I want to tell something to you," Mr. Shi says, and Madam flashes an eager smile. Mr. Shi shifts on the bench, and says in English, "I was not a rocket scientist."

Madam nods hard. Mr. Shi looks at her, and then looks away. "*I was not a rocket scientist because of a woman. The only thing we did was talk. Nothing wrong with talking, you would imagine, but no, talking between a married man and an unmarried girl was not accepted. That's how sad our time was back then.*" Yes, sad is the word, not crazy as young people use to talk about that period. "*One would always want to talk, even when not talking was part of our training.*" And talking, such a commonplace thing, but how people got addicted to it! Their talking started from five minutes of break in the office, and later they sat in the cafeteria and talked the whole lunch break. They talked about their hope and excitement in the grand history they were taking part in, of building the first rocket for their young communist mother.

"*Once you started talking, you talked more, and more. It*

was different than going home and talking to your wife be-cause you didn't have to hide anything. We talked about our own lives, of course. Talking is like riding with an unreined horse, you don't know where you end up and you don't have to think about it. That's what our talking was like, but we weren't having an affair as they said. We were never in love," Mr. Shi says, and then, for a short moment, is confused by his own words. What kind of love is he talking about? Surely they were in love, not the love they were suspected of having—he always kept a respectful distance, their hands never touched. But a love in which they talked freely, a love in which their minds touched—wasn't it love, too? Wasn't it how his daugh-ter ended her marriage, because of all the talking with an-other man? Mr. Shi shifts on the bench, and starts to sweat despite the cool breeze of October. He insisted they were in-nocent when they were accused of having an affair; he ap-pealed for her when she was sent down to a provincial town. She was a good puncher, but a puncher was always easier to train. He was, however, promised to remain in the position on the condition that he publicly admitted his love affair and gave a self-criticism. He refused because he believed he was wronged. *"I stopped being a rocket scientist at thirty-two. Never was I involved in any research after that, but everything at work was confidential so the wife didn't know."* At least that was what he thought until the previous night. He was as-signed to the lowest position that could happen to someone with his training—he decorated offices for the birthdays of Chairman Mao and the Party; he wheeled the notebooks and paperwork from one research group to the other; in the evening he collected his colleagues' notebooks and paper-work, logged them in, and locked them in the file cabinet in the presence of two security guards. He maintained his dignity at work, and went home to his wife as a preoccupied and silent rocket scientist. He looked away from the questions in his wife's eyes until the questions disappeared one day; he watched his daughter grow up, quiet and understanding as his wife was, a good girl, a good woman. Thirty-two guards he worked with during his career, young men in uniforms and carrying empty holsters on their belts, but the bayonets on their rifles were real.

But then, there was no other choice for him. The decision he made—wasn't it out of loyalty to the wife, and to the other woman? How could he have admitted the love affair, hurt his good wife, and remained a selfish rocket scientist— or, even more impossible, given up a career, a wife, and a two-year-old daughter for the not so glorious desire to spend a lifetime with another woman? *"It is what we sacrifice that makes life meaningful"*—Mr. Shi says the line that was often repeated in their training. He shakes his head hard. A foreign country gives one foreign thoughts, he thinks. For an old man like him, it is not healthy to ponder too much over memory. A good man should live in the present moment, with Madam, a dear friend sitting next to him, holding up a perfect golden ginkgo leaf to the sunshine for him to see.

Acknowledgments

I am deeply grateful to Kate Medina, my editor, and Richard Abate, my agent, for their trust, insight, and support; Kate Lee and Danielle Posen for all the hard work; editors who have taken risks on a new voice: Brigid Hughes, Cressida Leyshon, Deborah Treisman, Don Lee, Alex Linklater, Michael Ray, Linda Swanson-Davies, Susan Burmeister-Brown, and David Hamilton; the Paris Review Foundation and the Medway Institute for their generosity in offering space and time for this project; and Connie Brothers, whom I admire for countless reasons.

To teachers and writers whose wisdom has inspired me in the past two years: Marilynne Robinson, Frank Conroy, Edward Carey, and Stuart Dybek.

To friends for their support: Chen Reis, Amy Leach, Jebediah Reed, Kerry Reilly, Paul Ingram, Marilyn Abildskov, Katherine Bell, Timothy O'Sullivan, and Anne O'Reilly.

To my family for believing in everything I do.

Endless gratitude to the following people, who have changed my life: James Alan McPherson, my mentor; Barbara Bryan, my forever first reader; and Aviya Kushner, the enhancer of everything good in the world.

A
THOUSAND
YEARS
OF
GOOD
PRAYERS

Yiyun Li

A Reader's Guide

A Conversation with Yiyun Li

RANDOM HOUSE READER'S CIRCLE: *A Thousand Years of Good Prayers* presents readers with a stunning vision of China, past and present. When you think of your homeland, what thoughts or images come to mind? What are your feelings about China today?

YIYUN LI: I have always said that there are two Chinas. The first is a country filled with people, like my family and many others, who try to lead serious and meaningful lives despite the political, economic and cultural dilemmas they face. The second is a country with a government controlled by one party, made rich from corruption and injustice. I love the first China but do not love the second. So when I think about China today, I always have mixed feelings.

RHRC: When did you come to America, and what brought you here?

YL: I came to America in 1996 to attend the University of Iowa. I had planned to pursue a Ph.D. in immunology and hoped to stay in the medical science field as a researcher.

RHRC: But instead of becoming an immunologist, you became a writer—that is quite a switch! How did that happen?

YL: I had never thought of becoming a writer nor had I written anything before I came to Iowa. But once there I stumbled into a community writing class, which led to more writing classes, and I began to seriously consider changing my career.

RHRC: Such a career change must have been quite daunting. What inspired you to actually pursue writing? Did you have a literary role model or teacher, who encouraged you along the way?

YL: Several teachers early on were very encouraging and supportive, among them the Pulitzer Prize–winner James Alan McPherson, a great mentor and friend. When he read my first story, "Immortality," he became so excited that he actually tracked me down through a friend. He asked her to bring me two things: a present for my baby (I was seven months pregnant when I workshopped the story with him), and a message saying I was a great writer and that I had to keep writing. From that moment on I had no doubt that I wanted to write, and that I wanted to write well.

My literary role model is William Trevor, a great writer himself and a true gentleman. I always consider him my most important teacher in writing. I read his work again and again to get to my own voice.

RHRC: Speaking about your own voice and approach, how do you go about constructing a story? What process do you go through, to imagine the characters, structure, and plotline?

YL: I like to ask myself what kind of character would do certain things that other people would not do. For instance, I once saw a news clip that reported a beggar coming into a crowded marketplace with a sign: "If you give me ten yuan, I will let you cut me once; if you finish my life in one cut, you don't owe me anything." It was just one of the hundreds of little tales we hear and see every day, but I could not forget the beggar. In my mind, I kept imagining a woman who would come forward and cut the beggar with all justification and tenderness. What kind of character would do this? I thought about this and eventually the character Sansan (from "Love in the Marketplace") came to me. Most of my stories come this way, with a minor character (sometimes very minor) as a seed for imagination.

RHRC: I was struck by a wonderful line in the title story about the power of a new language. As Mr. Shi's daughter says, a new language "makes you a new person." Did you find this to be true when you began writing in English?

YL: Absolutely. For me, writing in English is the most liberating experience. In English, I am free to express things that I would have consciously censored—both out of political pressure and cultural pressure—had I been writing in Chinese.

RHRC: The "American dream" is a prevalent theme in your work. What does it mean to you personally, and also in your storytelling?

YL: For me, the American dream meant that I could pick up writing and become a writer, something I had never dared to dream before coming here. For my characters, it means freedom to escape totalitarian control on many different levels—from parental supervision to the ideological control of the Communist party.

RHRC: The stories in this collection are infused with aphorism and mythology. Where did you learn these wise and wonderful proverbs?

YL: Most of them I inherited from Chinese tradition and translated into English. Someone at a reading once said that he counted more than sixty of these sayings and I was quite surprised by the number. A lot of them are used in dialogue, which is how Chinese speak: full of proverbs and references to mythology. I used these to make the dialogue more genuine.

RHRC: Along those lines, what is your own favorite adage about life?

YL: There is a saying in Chinese: For someone to achieve anything, he has to first work as hard as he can; whether he is allowed the achievement, however, is determined afterwards by the heavenly power. I think the saying reflects how I feel about life and my characters. Several readers have commented on the fatalism of many of the characters in the stories, and I think that the fatalism came with my belief in this Chinese saying.

RHRC: Are you working on anything new?

YL: I am working on a novel set in China in 1979. It tells the story of the disintegration of a community after a public execution of a female political prisoner.

RHRC: America's history with China is complex, to say the least, and will be a defining relationship for the world of the twenty-first century. What do you think Americans should know about China that they might not already know? On the other hand, what do you think the Chinese should know about Americans?

YL: One time, I met two old women in the street here in America who read "Extra" and loved the story. They said to me, "we both agreed we could be Granny Lin." Another time someone told me that after reading "The Princess of Nebraska," he realized every Chinese graduate student he walked past in the street might have a rich story. These are the things that I think people in both countries tend to forget—that deep down we are all human beings, and the pains and joys we have are the same. In a way, I think the two countries are set up in the public view as competitors, which can lead some Americans and Chinese to feel wariness or animosity toward one another. But in the end, people here in America are like what you will find in China, too.

Questions and Topics for Discussion

For "Extra"

1. Consider Granny Lin and Kang. How is each an "extra"? What explains their bond?

2. Granny Lin cherishes her time with Kang as her "brief love story" (p. 22). What does she mean by this? Granny Lin also believes that "to love someone is to want to please him, even when one is not able to" (p. 19). How does this hold true in her friendship with Kang? How would you describe what it means to truly love someone?

3. Why does Granny Lin think the truth is futile? Discuss her reaction to Old Tang's death, and to Kang's disappearance. Why doesn't Granny defend herself? How do other characters in *A Thousand Years of Good Prayers* view the possibility for achieving truth and justice?

For "After A Life"

4. Why did Jian's birth turn the Sus's relationship cold, although the challenge of Beibei's condition did not? Why were Mr. and Mrs. Su able to share misfortune, but not happiness?

5. Imagine the questions that Mr. Su never gathered the courage to ask Mrs. Su. What might he want to ask her, in his deepest heart? Why does he decide, instead, that "things unsaid had better remain so" (p. 40)?

6. Discuss the theme of shame in "After a Life," and the many forms it takes in both the Su and Fong families. Does anyone overcome the weight of shame? Who deals with it best? Who hides it and remains imprisoned by it? What roles do honor and dishonor play throughout the entire collection of stories?

For "Immortality"

7. Describe the identity of the narrator of "Immortality." What atmosphere does this collective voice create?

8. Assess the complex attitudes of the people toward the Great Papas, the dictator, and the impersonator. How are these cultural figures—heroes and villains both—"larger than the universe" (p. 53) yet vulnerable to time? Do they achieve immortality in the hearts and minds of the people?

9. Yiyun Li presents the history of China through aphorism, mythology and storytelling. What does one gain from such a literary portrayal that one does not through history books?

For "The Princess of Nebraska"

10. "The Princess of Nebraska" is set in the heartland of America, during a small street parade. Discuss the juxtaposition of each character's life in China with his or her new experiences in America. How do they each react in this new environment?

11. Sasha believes that "moving on" (p. 69) is an American concept that suits her well. Do you agree that Americans have a unique ability to start fresh and forget the past? Do you see this optimism reflected in other cultures, or would you agree that it is an American outlook? Later, Sasha says Americans are "born to be themselves, naïve and contented with their naivety" (p. 78). Describe the insights behind this appraisal. Do you agree or disagree? What does this story reveal about Chinese and American psyches, and how do these revelations resonate throughout the entire book?

12. At the end of "The Princess of Nebraska," what do you think Sasha decides to do about the baby?

For "Love in the Marketplace"

13. Why does Sansan love the movie *Casablanca* so dearly? In what ways does it encompass "all she wants to teach the students about life?" (p. 95)

14. Discuss Sansan's sacrifice. Did she act virtuously or foolishly? What lies beneath her fierce attachment to the notion of her own "nobleness" (p. 102)? Later, why is Sansan so tenderly affected by the beggar in the marketplace, and his "promise"?

For "Son"

15. Think about Sansan in "Love in the Marketplace," Han in "Son," and Mr. Shi's daughter in "A Thousand Years of Good Prayers." How are the children of this generation in China, now adults, breaking away from the traditions of, and duties to, their parents?

16. What moves Han to reveal the long-kept secret of his sexuality to his mother? Were you surprised by her reaction? Is Han's mother as "traditional" as he believes?

For "The Arrangement"

17. Why does Ruolan's mother refuse a divorce? What is the "arrangement" that she has worked out with Uncle Bing and Ruolan's father?

18. Uncle Bing says he's "one of those fools who puts a magic leaf in front of his eyes and then stops seeing mountains and seas" (p. 143). What does this mean? Have you ever fallen victim to a similar preoccupation?

For "Death Is Not A Bad Joke If Told The Right Way"

19. What does Mrs. Pang mean when she says "Nobody knows who he will become tomorrow?" (p. 152) What does this sentiment reveal about life in China?

20. Discuss the importance of Mr. Du's orchids. Why is Mr. Du happy when they go out of fashion? What do the orchids mean to him?

21. Do you think Mrs. Pang have been proud of Mr. Pang at the end of his life, as the girl believes?

For "Persimmons"

22. Describe the view of life and death that the villagers hold. Is existence controlled by fate? God? Man? Consider, also, their attitude toward the possibility for justice.

For "A Thousand Years of Good Prayers"

23. Describe the emotional barriers to communication in "A Thousand Years of Good Prayers." Are Mr. Bing and his daughter able to express their feelings? Why? Does language hinder or promote their abilities? How does the power to communicate in a new language make one "a new person" (p. 199)?

24. Yiyun Li sets many of her stories in her homeland of China. What is the spirit of the people like there? What mood pervades the workers' lives? How would you describe the way characters such as Granny Kang, Mr. and Mrs. Su, Sansan, and Mr. Du, respond to adversity?

25. Discuss your impressions of the world and the characters that Yiyun Li has created. Draw comparisons and contrasts between the stories in the collection as a whole. Which story is the most memorable or the most powerful for you and why? What themes are woven throughout the entire collection? What images or feelings emerge when you think of the collection as a whole?

Read on for an excerpt from
Gold Boy, Emerald Girl
by Yiyun Li

Published by Random House

Gold Boy, Emerald Girl

HE WAS RAISED by his mother alone, as she was by her father. She wondered if his mother, who had set up their date, had told him about that.

Siyu was thirty-eight, and the man, Hanfeng, was forty-four. Siyu's father, after supporting her through college, had remarried, choosing a woman thirty years his junior. The woman had a young son from her previous marriage, whom Siyu's father had taken on as his responsibility. The boy was now in his last year of high school, and Siyu, having told her father many times that he deserved peace and simplicity, maintained a respectful distance from his new family. Each year she spent New Year's Eve, and sometimes other holidays, with Hanfeng's mother, who had been her zoology professor in college. There was no way to predict when the older woman would be in the mood to invite Siyu, so she tried to keep herself uncommitted, which meant that most of the holidays she spent alone.

"Professor Dai must miss her students these days," Siyu said after she and Hanfeng had exchanged greetings, although she knew it was not the students that his mother missed but the white skulls of mammals and birds on her office shelves, the drawers filled with scalpels and clamps and tweezers that she had cleaned and maintained with care, and the fact that she could mask her indifference to the human species with her devotion to animals. The first time Siyu had seen Professor Dai, on a campus tour during the opening week of college, the older woman had been following a strutting owl down a dimly lit hallway; she paid little attention to the group of new students, and stooped slightly the whole time, as if she were the mother of a toddler and had to watch out for minor accidents. When a boy stepped over to take a closer look at the owl, she scooped up the bird and glared at him before striding away.

"Retirement is a strange thing for her," Hanfeng said. His mother had always despised women who grabbed every opportunity to matchmake, but within days of his return to China she had mentioned a former student she thought he should meet. His mother did not say much else, but he could sense that it was marriage she was thinking about. Twenty years of living away from her had not changed that in him: He always knew what was on her mind before she said it, and he wondered if she was ever aware of that.

The teahouse where Hanfeng and Siyu were meeting, at a hillside pavilion in the Summer Palace, had been chosen by his mother, and she had suggested that they also take a long stroll along the lakefront. It was early March. The day turned out overcast and windy, and secretly Hanfeng hoped that the wind would not die down, so they could forgo the romantic walk. He wondered if Siyu was wishing for a different scenario. He could not yet read much from her face. She smiled courteously as she gave him a few facts about White Peony, the tea she had ordered for them both, but the smile and the words seemed to come with effort, as if her interest in interacting with him could easily fade. Her body was slender, and her hair, black with noticeable strands of gray, was kept straight and at shoulder length. He wondered why the woman, who was beautiful in an unassuming way, had never married.

"Do you find Beijing a different city now?" Siyu said. It must be a question that he was asked all the time, but it would not do anyone any harm, she thought. It was not the first time that Siyu had been set up with a stranger—since she had turned twenty, neighbors and acquaintances, pitying her for not having a mother to fuss over her future, had taken it as their responsibility to find a husband for her—but with those men she had known from the beginning that she would not bother trying to impress them. Over the years, she had developed a reputation as unmatchable, and nowadays only the most persistent of the matchmakers would mention a widower or a divorcé, in his fifties or sometimes sixties, as a possible solution. The first time such a prospect was presented in an enthusiastic speech, Siyu had the odd feeling that she was now expected to marry her father; only later did she realize that she was no longer a young woman.

Siyu worked as a librarian in a zoology institute, and her life had not changed much from that of a college student. In her mind, she might still be the eighteen-year-old who had set her alarm clock early so that by six o'clock she would be sitting on the bench under an ancient ginkgo tree in front of the biology building. At half past six, Professor Dai would arrive on her bicycle—a tall, rusty, heavy-built one that would have better suited a peasant or a street peddler—and she would nod at Siyu almost imperceptibly as she locked it up. It had taken two years for Professor Dai to cross the courtyard and ask Siyu about the thick volume she had been reading every day. Charles Dickens, Siyu replied, and then added that she was trying to memorize *Great Expectations*. Professor Dai nodded, expressing neither surprise nor curiosity at the task that had already made Siyu an eccentric in the eyes of her classmates. Siyu did not explain to them that her grandfather—her mother's father, whom she had never met—had once memorized volumes of Dickens on the small balcony of a Shanghai flat, a feat that had eventually led him, before the liberation, to a high position in a bank run by Englishmen. It was Dickens who had in the end killed Siyu's mother: As a daughter of the British capitalists' loyal lapdog, she had hanged herself when her own daughter was four months of age, barely old enough to be weaned.

Hanfeng looked at Siyu's face, detecting a familiar absentmindedness. His mother, too, asked him questions to which she seemed scarcely interested in knowing the answers. He wondered if this happened to women who lived by themselves. "Too many cars," he replied, nonetheless—the standard response he gave when asked about his impression of Beijing these days. "I miss the bicycles."

Hanfeng had returned from the States a month earlier. He had told his former colleagues in San Francisco about his intention to settle down in China, and they had joked about moving with him and becoming the forty-niners of the new gold rush. He went along with the joke, making up ambitious business plans that he knew he would not carry out. His mother was getting old, he explained to his friends; the thought that he, too, was no longer a young man in need of adventures he kept to himself. Semiretired was how he liked to think of his situation, but within days of returning to Beijing he realized that what he had made in the States at the tail end of the dot-com bubble would not be sufficient to support a life of idleness, as he had hoped. Still, he was not eager to go out and seek employment. He deposited half his money into his mother's account and told her that he would take a break; she did not ask about his plans, in the same way that she had not questioned his decision to leave or to come home.

At seventy-one, his mother was as independent as ever, and she loathed most activities that a woman her age enjoyed: taking morning walks with a companion, gossiping and bargaining at the marketplace, watching soap operas in the afternoon. Hanfeng had never wondered how his mother spent her days in retirement until his return, when, all of a sudden, the three-bedroom flat that must have seemed empty to her became crowded. He had been the one to cook for the two of them when he was a boy, dividing the meals in half and eating his portion alone; his mother, her preoccupation with her research a ready excuse, had eaten at odd hours then. Since his return, he had taken over the cooking again, and now that neither of them was eager to go out into the world to fulfill any duty, they ate together.

The idea of renting a flat had occurred to Hanfeng, but as soon as the thought formed he dismissed it as a waste: He had left for America right after college, a move intended to claim a place for himself—a whole continent, in the end, as in twenty years he had drifted from New York to Montreal, then Vancouver, and later San Francisco—and a life that had to be lived away from a mother, but with the return to China he no longer felt the urgency to have his own place. Freedom is like restaurant food, he once told an old friend in the States, and one can lose one's appetite for even the best restaurants. Pure nonsense, replied his friend, who, unlike Hanfeng, had long ago settled down with a partner, a house, and two dogs, and talked of adopting a baby. Take a break, he said, urging Hanfeng to return to California after he refreshed himself with his homemade dumplings and noodles. Hanfeng, however, could envision himself living a bachelor's life in his mother's flat, reading the same newspapers and comparing notes on the stories that interested them both, wandering freely through the flat when she went out for her piano lessons twice a week.

The piano was the only thing that kept his mother actively engaged with the world. Soon after Hanfeng's return, she had asked him to go to a recital she was playing in, at a local music school. It was attended by men and women Hanfeng's age, who seemed nervous when their well-trained and nicely dressed children took the stage. His mother was the only one who went up without a puppetlike show. She gazed at the sheets of music for a long moment, then started to pound on the keys with a seriousness that took Hanfeng by surprise. He had thought the piano was merely a retirement pastime for his mother, and had protested mildly when she mentioned that her goal was to be good enough one day to play four-hand with him. Hanfeng had not told her that he was no longer playing, even though a rented piano had always been the first piece of furniture to fill an empty flat in each city he moved to. Small children giggled in the audience, and a few older ones smirked, pitying the old woman for her stiff arthritic fingers, which would never again be as good and agile as theirs. Some parents shook their heads at their children disapprovingly, and it occurred to Hanfeng that he was becoming a parent for his mother, that he would be the one to protect her from the hostility of the world.

The thought baffled him. His mother had always been a headstrong woman, and with her grayish-white mane and unsmiling face, she appeared as regal and intimidating as she had ever been. Still, seeing her through other people's eyes, Hanfeng realized that all that made her who she was—the decades of solitude in her widowhood, her coldness to the prying eyes of people who tried to mask their nosiness with friendliness, and her faith in the notion of living one's own life without having to go out of one's way for other people—could be deemed pointless and laughable. Perhaps the same could be said of any living creature: a caterpillar chewing on a leaf, unaware of the beak of an approaching bird; an egret mesmerized by its reflection in a pond, as if it were the master of the universe; or Hanfeng's own folly of repeating the same pattern of hope and heartbreak, hoping despite heartbreak.

Siyu asked a few more questions, and Hanfeng replied. When there was nothing much left to say, he curled his fingers around the teacup and studied its shape, and Siyu pictured him as a young boy, spreading his slender fingers on the cold keys of a piano. His mother must have told him, when he complained about the open windows in the winter, that playing would keep the blood circulating in his hands. Siyu did not know why she imagined that; it was as unfounded as all the other things she had made up about him. In Professor Dai's flat, there were framed snapshots of Hanfeng playing in piano contests at five, eight, ten, fifteen. There were snapshots of him when he had first arrived in America, with his bright-colored T-shirt, long and flying hair, and broad smile, as picturesque and unreal as the Statue of Liberty in the background.

Siyu had been eighteen when she first saw those photographs, when she was sent as a representative from her class to deliver a New Year's present to Professor Dai. No one had wanted that job; Professor Dai's coldness was known to be hurtful, and it made sense that Siyu, with her mild eccentricity, would be the one chosen. But that day, to Siyu's surprise, Professor Dai did not simply dismiss her from the doorway, even though she immediately placed the present, a framed painting of a golden carp, next to the wastebasket. Instead, Professor Dai invited Siyu into the flat, moved the papers that covered the dining table onto the piano bench, and let Siyu sit while she went to the kitchen to make tea. Her son was the one who played the piano, Professor Dai answered when Siyu asked, and pointed out the pictures of Hanfeng. Very vaguely, Siyu had thought that he was the kind of boy she would like to have as a boyfriend, a prize badge that she could wear to make other girls jealous. Years later, she knew it was not the thought of the boy that had made her wait on the bench outside the biology building in the mornings during college; nor was he the reason she continued to befriend Professor Dai in a manner allowed by the older woman. Occasionally, Siyu would carefully study the pictures of Hanfeng in Professor Dai's flat, and when they ran out of things to say about animals she would ask about his life in America. When Professor Dai called and asked her to meet Hanfeng, Siyu wondered if the matchmaking had come as a result of a beguiling impression she had left of her interest in a good-looking bachelor.

The waitress came to offer a fresh pot of tea. Hanfeng turned to Siyu and asked her if she was ready to leave. They had spent almost an hour talking, and he had fulfilled his mother's wish without humiliating the woman with his lack of interest. Siyu looked out the window at the willow trees, their branches waving like unruly hair in the wind. Not a great day for a walk, Hanfeng said. Siyu agreed, then asked him if he needed a ride.

"I'll take a cab home," he said.

"I'm driving past your mother's place, in any case," Siyu said. Her own flat, a small studio that she rented from a retired couple, was only minutes from Professor Dai's flat, but Siyu thought she would appear too eager if she mentioned that.

Hanfeng wished that he had made up an excuse—a lunch

with a friend in another district; an exhibition or a film to see—
but it was too late to correct himself now.

A WEEK LATER, Hanfeng's mother asked him if he planned to
see Siyu again. They had finished their breakfast and were reading that morning's newspapers, plates and bowls scattered on the
table between them. Hanfeng's mother did not raise her eyes
from the page as she asked, but he knew the question was not as
haphazard as it seemed. Should he? he replied.

"Do you dislike her?"

It took more than an hour over tea for him to say that he dis-
liked a woman, Hanfeng thought, but he just shook his head
slightly. He was not surprised by his mother's question. *Do you
dislike piano?* she had asked, when he wanted to give up the in-
strument at twelve for games that he could play with boys his
age; *Do you dislike engineering?*, when he thought of pursuing a
literature degree in college rather than the one she had chosen for
him. Before he left China, she told him that she might not have
been a good mother in the worldly sense, but she considered herself successful in having given him two things: practical skills
with which to earn a living, and music as the only trustworthy
companion and consolation for his soul. Twenty-three, and in
love with a childhood friend who was dating a chirpy girl, Hanfeng did not believe that either of his mother's gifts would in any
way contribute to his happiness. America, at first glance, seemed
a happy enough place, and when his friend called with the news
of his engagement, Hanfeng sought out companions. All he
wanted was to have some fun, he replied when more was asked
of him; "have fun"—?wasn't that the phrase that replaced words
of farewell in many Americans' lexicon? But eventually the reply

came back to taunt him: I thought we would have some fun and that's all, his last lover had said, a Chinese boy, a new immigrant, as Hanfeng himself had once been, whom Hanfeng had helped support through college.

He should ask Siyu out to a movie, his mother suggested, or a concert. When he showed a lukewarm reaction, she said, "Or ask her to have dinner with us here."

"Wouldn't that be too quick?" Hanfeng said. Even though Siyu had been introduced to him by his mother, a dinner invitation, after meeting only once, seemed to imply an approval of sorts from both him and his mother.

"She is not a stranger," his mother replied, and proceeded to check the calendar on the kitchen wall. Saturday was a good day, she said, and when Hanfeng questioned Siyu's availability at such short notice, his concerns were dismissed. "She'll rearrange her schedule if she has to," his mother said, and wrote down the date and Siyu's number on a piece of scrap paper.

Hanfeng wondered if Siyu had felt similar pressure from his mother. What would she have said to Siyu—*I would like you to date my son?* Knowing his mother, he wondered if she had simply mentioned that her son needed a wife and that she thought Siyu would be the right person for the role. "Why has she never married?" he asked.

"I imagine for the obvious reason of not having felt the need to get married."

"Does she want to get married now?" Hanfeng said. He had expected his mother to reply that Siyu had not met the right person—and then he could have questioned why his mother thought him a good choice for her.

"She ?didn't say no to the date last time, no?"

When Hanfeng called Siyu to invite her to dinner, the line was quiet for a moment. He waited for her to find an excuse to turn down the invitation, or, better still, to tell him that she had obliged his mother with their last meeting and the sensible thing to do now was to make their mutual disinterest known to his mother. Instead, Siyu asked him if they could possibly meet once more before the dinner. Anytime after she got off from work would do, she said. He wondered why she needed to see him when all could be settled on the phone, but he agreed to a late-afternoon meeting that day.

There was a power outage at the coffee shop where Siyu had suggested they meet. Apart from the light of a few candles on the counter, the inside of the shop, a long, narrow rectangle, was almost pitch-black. Siyu, who had arrived a few minutes earlier and taken a seat by the only window, explained to Hanfeng that the place was always quiet, and more so today, as the coffeemakers were not hissing. A sulky young girl placed a pot of tea and two cups heavily on the table. Siyu apologized for the shop's unfriendliness after the girl returned to the counter. "I'm about their only regular customer, but for three years no one has acknowledged me," she said.

"Why do you still come here?"

"It's quiet. I can assure you it's not easy to find a quiet place like this in Beijing," Siyu said. "My theory is that the proprietress is a rich man's mistress. She does not want the shop to make money for him, and he cannot close it, because it was his present to her."

Hanfeng looked around, but no one was there besides the girl at the counter. "They seem to hire unhappy people," he said.

"The proprietress is a beautiful woman," Siyu said. Hanfeng nodded. He had no further questions, and she could see that he was one of those people who would not return to the place. She wished she could tell him that, apart from the beauty of the woman who once in a while showed up at the coffee shop with an air of authority, there was little evidence to support her guess. Yet there had to be an explanation for the sad, lifeless appearance of the shop. She thought of telling him this, but he was part of the world that did not seek her explanations. The world had made up its mind about her oddity in her spinsterhood.

They sat in silence for a moment. In another place, a more romantic setting, lovers' murmurs would have been well masked by soft jazz coming from hidden speakers, their faces illuminated by candlelight, but here there was no music and the candles were lit out of necessity. The idea of getting to know Hanfeng better before having dinner with him and his mother seemed, like all the other ideas that had occurred to Siyu, a regrettable mistake. When he did not help find a harmless topic of discussion, she asked him if he was aware of his mother's wish to see him get married.

"I suppose all mothers worry about their children's marriage status," Hanfeng said vaguely. He had thought that his mother had long ago accepted who he was; when he had visited in the past, she had never pressed for any details of his American life, sparing him the pain of explaining himself. "Doesn't your mother?"

She had no right to feel let down, Siyu thought. Nevertheless, it disappointed her that Professor Dai had not told him much about her. That she had been raised by her father was, from a young age, the first thing people said of her. "I never met my mother," she said. "My father brought me up by himself."

Hanfeng looked up at her. Before he could form an apology, she said there was no need for one. She had grown up not knowing her loss, so there had not been any real loss. She wondered if that was how Hanfeng thought of his father. Professor Dai had never mentioned her late husband, but Siyu had once had a summer job in the department office, and had heard other professors and the secretaries talk about how he had died in a snowstorm when his bicycle skidded in front of a bus. An accident that no one could be blamed for, but Siyu had sensed the others' disapproval of Professor Dai, as if she were partially responsible for the unfair fate that befell the man; the dead husband, by contrast, was always praised as the gentlest person.

"What was it like to grow up with only a father?" Hanfeng asked. He had little recollection of his father, but there were photographs, taken when Hanfeng had turned a hundred days, six months, one year, and then two years old. In all four pictures, he was flanked by his parents, who looked serious and attentive. They would have been called "gold boy" and "emerald girl" at their wedding, enviable for their matching good looks. It must have been his father's idea to have a family picture taken at every milestone of his life, since after his father's death Hanfeng had never been in the same photograph as his mother.

Siyu replied that she imagined it was not very different from growing up with only a mother. There was no other parent to whom they could compare the one they had, and love did not have to be balanced and divided between two people; the claiming of loyalty was unnecessary. Siyu did not say these things, but there was a gentleness in Hanfeng's eyes where before there had been only aloofness, and she knew that he understood.

Hanfeng turned away from Siyu's gaze and looked out the window. A woman in a heavy ?mud-?colored coat was riding a bicycle and threading through the long line of cars in the street. A young child, bundled up in a gray shawl, so that its gender could not be determined, sat on a bamboo chair affixed to the back rack of the bicycle, as unfazed as the mother was by the impatient honking of drivers around them. Hanfeng pointed out the child to Siyu, knowing that both of them had traveled the streets of Beijing in that way, he behind his mother, she her father.

After the woman and her child had disappeared from sight, Siyu said that when she started to ride her bicycle to school at twelve, her father would get up every morning and run after her until she reached the school gate. She used to be ashamed of being the only one escorted to school by a running father, but she could never say no to him.

"He must be the most loving father in the world," Hanfeng said.

Siyu nodded. A door behind the counter opened and then closed, and for a moment it seemed that the flickering candles would be extinguished. She had had to squeeze the hand brake often on the downhill ride to the school so that her father's panting would not be so loud that other people took notice, and only when she was much older did she realize that her father had insisted on running beside her so that she would not become one of the wild youngsters who sped and broke an arm or a skull in an accident. She had always been aware of his love for her and for her mother, even though he had not said much, but in the end she had been the one to make up grand excuses for her absence. You're still my only daughter, he said to her when she decided not to attend his wedding; you're part of the family, he said when she told him that she would not be coming home for the Lunar New Year. He did not need her to complicate his life, she replied, knowing that he would stoically accept her proposal of a monthly lunch as their only way of remaining father and daughter.

Ungrateful and coldhearted she must seem in the eyes of old neighbors and family friends, but how could she stay in his sight when she was going through her life with a reckless speed known only to herself, all because of a love she could not explain and did not have the right to claim in the first place? I wonder if I made a mistake by bringing you up alone, her father had said to her at their most recent lunch, taking it as his failure that she had not found a husband. I was afraid of what a stepmother would do to a girl, but perhaps a woman would have made a difference, he said, less guarded and more talkative now in his old age. Siyu shook her head and denied that he had anything to regret. That she had grown up without a mother could be a ready explanation for anything—her oddness in her teenage years, her choice of an unremarkable job despite her excellence in schoolwork, her singleness. Were people to know her secret, they might easily conclude that she had spent her life looking for a mother in her love of an older woman, but Siyu did not believe that things would have turned out any differently had she had a mother.

A beautiful and sad woman, Hanfeng thought as he looked at Siyu's face. As beautiful and sad a woman, perhaps, as his mother had once been. Could this account for his mother's wish for a marriage between Siyu and him? Hanfeng had been surprised, at first, that a former student would remain close to his mother. She had not been the kind to pick favorites among her students; nor had she ever encouraged any personal interaction with them, as far as he knew, though he could see why Siyu, motherless and with a gentle and loving father, might seek out a professor despite, or perhaps because of, her sternness. But Siyu seemed to know his mother only in a peripheral way, as a pupil, and Hanfeng wondered if this was why his mother had allowed the younger woman to remain a friend. When Hanfeng was ten, a woman had come from a southern province to see his mother. An unannounced visit, he could tell, when his mother had returned home in the evening and found him shelling peas alongside the guest, their knees almost touching, on two low stools. The woman, who had told Hanfeng that she was a very old friend of his mother's and was planning to stay with them for a week, left the next morning before he awoke. He was puzzled but intuitively knew not to ask his mother about it. Still, the image of the woman's face, pale at the sight of his mother, and her hands, which let the peas fall into the pile of shells, stayed with Hanfeng. He could not pinpoint when he understood that there had been betrayals between the two friends, but by the time he left home for college he knew that he would never learn the true story, his mother having long ago decided to live alone with the secret until her death.

AT THE DINNER, both Siyu and Hanfeng felt a shyness around each other, but Professor Dai did not let the awkwardness deter her. "When you are young, you marry for passion," she said, looking first at her son and then at her future daughter-in-law. "When you're older, you marry for companionship."

Hanfeng glanced down at his plate. One day she would die, his mother had said to him the night before, after he had listened to her stumble through a Chopin piece on the piano. There was nothing to grieve about in her death, but she would like to see that he did not repeat her fate. Repeat? Hanfeng asked, pretending that he did not understand and knowing that she could see through him. She would like him to marry Siyu, his mother had said. There were many ways to maintain a marriage, and she expected theirs to be far from the worst.

The same message had been conveyed to Siyu, when Hanfeng was sent to buy a bottle of wine for dinner. She was helping Professor Dai lay the table, and when she looked over, the older woman paired the chopsticks without meeting her eyes. Siyu had never mentioned the strangers she had been matched up with over the years, but one New Year's Eve, Professor Dai had told Siyu that she ?shouldn't get married if it was not what she wanted. They had just finished dinner, and sitting across the table from Professor Dai, Siyu could see the prints of bamboo leaves on the curtain lit up by the fireworks outside. Professor Dai had opened a bottle of wine that year, an unusual addition to the holiday meal, as neither of them was the type to celebrate. You could feel trapped by the wrong man, Professor Dai said. Her voice, softened by the wine, was less steely and almost inaudible beneath the booming of the fireworks. You would have to wish for his death every day of your marriage, she said, but once the wish was granted by a miracle, you would never be free of your own cruelty. Siyu listened, knowing that the older woman was talking about herself, knowing also that both of them would pretend to have forgotten the conversation after that night. Other conversations, on other New Year's Eves, were never mentioned again. One year, Siyu told Professor Dai about her mother's suicide; another year, Professor Dai mentioned that her son had no interest in marriage. Professor Dai's acknowledgment of Siyu's decision to purchase a secondhand car so that the older woman could avoid taking a crowded bus or enduring a chatty cabdriver was hinted at but not directly stated, and so was her gratitude for Siyu's alertness, when she failed to answer Siyu's weekly phone call and Siyu discovered the older woman on the floor by the piano, having suffered a stroke.

She had remained unmarried for Professor Dai, Siyu thought now, and she would, with her blessing, become a married woman. She would not wish for her husband's death, as his mother had, because the marriage, arranged as it was, would still be a love marriage. Siyu had wished to be a companion for Professor Dai in her old age, and her wish would now be granted, an unexpected gift from a stingy life.

"So this is an engagement dinner, then?" Hanfeng said, feeling that it was his duty to say something to avoid silence among the three of them. He doubted that he would feel any deficiency in his life without a wife, he had said the night before, and his mother had replied that Siyu was not the kind of woman who would take much away from him.

"We don't need any formality among us," Professor Dai said now, and told Siyu that she should move in at her earliest convenience instead of wasting money on rent. Siyu looked down the hallway, knowing that the room which served as a piano studio for Professor Dai would be converted into the third bedroom, the piano relocated to the living room. She could see herself standing by the window and listening to Hanfeng and Professor Dai play ?four-?hand, and she could see the day when she would replace Professor Dai on the piano bench, her husband patient with her inexperienced fingers. They were half orphans, and beyond that there was the love for his mother that they could share with no one else, he as a son who had once left but had now returned, she who had not left and would never leave. They were lonely and sad people, all three of them, and they would not make one another less sad, but they could, with great care, make a world that would accommodate their loneliness.

PHOTO: © YE RIN MOK

YIYUN LI is the recipient of numerous awards, including the PEN/Hemingway Award, the Frank O'Connor International Short Story Award, the *Guardian* First Book Award, and a MacArthur fellowship. Many of her stories have appeared in *The New Yorker*, which named her one of the top twenty writers under forty. She teaches at the University of California, Davis, and lives with her husband and two sons.

www.yiyunli.com

Chat.
Comment.
Connect.

Visit our online book club community at
www.randomhousereaderscircle.com

Chat
Meet fellow book lovers and discuss what you're reading.

Comment
Post reviews of books, ask—and answer—thought-provoking
questions, or give and receive book club ideas.

Connect
Find an author on tour, visit our author blog, or invite one of
our 150 available authors to chat with your group on the phone.

Explore
Also visit our site for discussion questions, excerpts, author
interviews, videos, free books, news on the latest releases,
and more.

Books are better with buddies.
www.RandomHouseReadersCircle.com